Unfinished Business

Barbara Marvin

(Joy B. Sister)

Copyright ©2013 Barbara Marvin
Book-broker Publishers of Florida,
Port Charlotte, FL 33980
Printed in the United States of America
All rights reserved
ISBN: **978-0-9894967-8-0**

To correspond or order additional copies
Call **941-474-1286**,
e-mail **cardinal ventures39@gmail.com**
or visit
facebook.com/Unfinishedbusinessbarbara

Unfinished Business

CHAPTER 1: December 2005

It was two weeks before Christmas and the weather in Florida was warm, sunny, and exactly what the snowbirds loved. But dark clouds were forming and weather changed fast in the Sunshine State.

Frankie had washed and waxed his truck right after lunch, although he knew the forecast predicted rain. The weathermen were usually right, but the metallic blue Ford pickup was his prized possession; he liked to keep it shiny and clean.

His well-worn Levi jeans were clean and his favorite denim shirt had been ironed. His dark brown hair was slicked back with a dab of his wife's hair gel.

Looking at himself in the rear view mirror, he saw the perfect image of a small time ranch hand. He was a young man with a wife and children and he considered himself lucky to have his job.

As caretaker for the Parnell ranch, he was responsible for four thousand acres, a few head of cattle and horses and little else, except to make sure no one trespassed on the property.

But last week he allowed three men to hunt on the ranch. He had been patrolling the ranch on his four-wheeler, just like he did every week. The wild boars had been having a field day rooting up the ground near the east pond. While checking the area one day he saw three men standing there. They had heard his vehicle and were watching him.

"Hey, can I help you?" he blurted out. "This is private property, no hunting here."

"We didn't realize this is private," said the man with tattoos on his neck. "Can you make an exception today, since we're already here? I'll make it worth your while." The man was looking straight at Frankie and hadn't moved or cracked a smile; the other men were staring at him also.

Frankie's eyes were riveted on the man's neck. He had never seen such a large and scary tattoo in his life. It was a half moon with a devil's face. The guy looked like a wrestler or something and Frankie just wanted to be gone. When Tattoo Man reached in his pocket for his wallet, Frankie saw more tattoos. All eight fingers had letters on them. The words HATE and LOVE were bold and black. Tattoo Man was the only one to speak, the other two men kept their eyes on him. He really wanted to be out of there. But it was Christmas and he could use a few extra dollars.

Tattoo Man pulled three one hundred dollar bills out of his well-worn wallet and held them up for Frankie to see.

"OK, but just this once, my boss will kill me if he finds out," Frankie said. And with shaky hands he took the bills and stuffed them in his pocket.

"He'll never hear it from us," Tattoo Man said and smiled for the first time.

Frankie turned the four-wheeler around and left the area, as fast as he could. "Phew! I wonder what they are up to." He wasn't good at remembering faces, but those he would never forget.

When he told his friend Jake what happened, he promised to never tell, and advised Frankie to not mention it to Mr. Parnell. "Why lose a good job over a few dollars?" he said.

Remembering that encounter made Frankie nervous even now, a week later.

"Already getting dark out, it's really going to storm," he said. "I hope I can pick up my check and run. Like that's going to happen," He was dismally aware of the changes in the weather. He could smell the rain coming.

The digital clock on the dash said 6:15. He expected to be right on time. Mr. Parnell had said be there at 6:30 and being punctual was a must. After all, he was picking up his Christmas bonus. Even though this was the third year he would collect, it was never routine for him.

His pick-up truck lumbered on and the odometer ticked off the miles. He could see the boss's place as he turned left off U.S. 41 at Mullet Bay road. The large wrought-iron gate with security cameras on either side seemed like overkill to him. But it opened when he punched in the four-digit number and that was all he cared about.

At the end of the drive was his boss's large house surrounded by a well-manicured lawn. As the breeze picked up, the palms lining the drive started to sway. Looking past the house he could see water through the trees and knew it was Mullet Bay. There were boats anchored in the bay, some decked out for the holiday and others that stood unadorned, their owners waiting for a better day for boating.

Slowly braking to a stop under the ivy-covered entrance, Frankie put the truck in park. After checking his reflection in the mirror one last time he jumped out. His six-foot frame was dwarfed by the huge door. It was metal with ironwork in the shape of ornate birds that looked like egrets standing in tall marshes.

Looking skyward, Frankie said a silent prayer to the rain gods to hold off just a little while longer.

Were the gods listening to a red-neck ranch hand like me? Probably not, but it was worth a shot. His heart raced; well, here goes nothing. He was breathing deep, trying to calm himself; his finger touched the door bell. And in seconds the door opened.

The maid let him in and led him to the library as usual. Frankie had never learned to read well and was intimidated by so many books, the high ceiling and the large paintings on the walls. On one side of the room there was a sofa for reading; on the opposite side a dark wood desk complemented the round table and chairs. An enormous Christmas tree stood in front of the floor-to-ceiling windows, facing the bay. It was decorated in gold with an angel on the top. He looked at the angel, smiled and said in a whisper, "Help me!"

Before he could decide which place to sit, Mr. P. entered. Cleveland Parnell was a big man who reminded Frankie of Lorne Greene, the actor who played Ben Cartwright on his favorite TV show, *Bonanza*.

Parnell immediately handed him an envelope, shook his hand, thanked him, wished him Merry Christmas and said something about being late to catch a plane. He then retreated, leaving Frankie alone.

The maid appeared immediately and led Frankie back the way he had come. Total time in the Parnell residence was about fifteen minutes. Customarily, his boss sat with him, if only for a short time. Sometimes they had a drink together. But Frankie wasn't disappointed with the short audience with his boss tonight. This short encounter could be the difference between getting home before it rained, and getting caught in this storm. Just maybe the rain gods were listening. Or was it the angel on top of the tree? He thought he saw her smile.

As he drove out of the compound, the red and green envelope burned a hole in his pocket. But he always waited to open it until he was home with Cary. He hoped it would put her in a better mood. She was miffed because he was going fishing with Jake early tomorrow. She wanted to go shopping, as usual, but she would just have to wait one more day.

The wrought-iron gate opened and he maneuvered through. At the corner he merged into traffic on US 41 and headed south. Traffic was lighter than it had been earlier; maybe the expected storm sent everyone scampering home, which was what he intended to do.

But tiny raindrops hitting the windshield were just the prelude of things to come. Within five minutes the dark skies showed no mercy. Rain pelted the truck like it was in a car wash. He could still see, but it wasn't comfortable.

"So much for getting home before the rain!" he said. "OK, Cary, I'm on my way, just sit tight." His wife had a real fear of thunderstorms. He wanted to stop and call her, but that would delay him and it would mean getting wet so he opted for staying dry.

He passed the last residential area; by now his was the only car he could see. He could barely make out the Mobil station up ahead. But he would be home soon. The headlights sliced through the night as Frankie turned off the highway and onto the familiar dirt road that would take him to his house. This road had a name, although the sign that had been put there many years before had seen its better days and was illegible.

His house was just a mile from the highway and most people never knew anyone lived there. He was beginning to feel uneasy driving. River Road was without street lights. The darkness was thick and heavy, it pressed in on all sides.

KABOOM! A flash of lightning was followed immediately by thunder; the rain never let up. Frankie's knuckles were white from gripping the wheel and his eyes raw from focusing through the rain on the road in front of him. The wipers moving back and forth on high were useless. Slowing even more and peering out, he could barely see the road.

"Just my luck," he moaned. "Fifteen minutes, fifteen minutes."

The dirt road was filling with water fast and turning to mud. Steering in the washed out ruts was difficult. In the dark he couldn't see the tops of the pines. Low-hanging branches from the many Brazilian pepper trees whipped at his truck.

I'll have to trim these trees tomorrow when I get home from fishing, he promised himself. It wasn't helping now. That edgy feeling just wouldn't go away. Was it the weather? KABOOM! Lightning and then thunder again. If it wasn't for the lightning, he wouldn't be able to see at all. Usually he could see the porch light from this area, right through the trees, but not tonight.

"Electricity may be out, no lights in the house at all. I should call Jake and cancel tomorrow. We can go another time."

KABOOM! He slowly pulled into the dirt drive as close to the house as possible. He cut the headlights and the engine, jumped from the truck and slammed the door. He landed squarely in the water that was already covering his yard. "Oh shit."

The house was in total darkness, he ran to the porch just as the lightning lit up the sky. The screen door squeaked when he opened it; the wooden inside door was stuck again. That happened every time it rained.

Putting his shoulder to the door he gave it a push. It opened and he stepped over the threshold. His hand easily found the light switch in the dark. He flipped it on and the lamp in the corner illuminated the room. The electricity wasn't out.

He hesitated. Something wasn't right—what was it? Something was wrong, what was that smell? The odor was stronger than the cedar Christmas tree standing in the corner with its few wrapped presents. His mind was screaming, but his body was frozen.

He took one small step away from the front door. Instantly his eyes fixed on the closed bedroom door. He was terrified. Why? What was wrong? Why was he terrified looking at the door? Oh no, that smell, what was it? His feet wanted to move but he wasn't going to follow. Something was wrong.

"Cary! Cary! Are you awake?" he shouted over the sound of the storm. His hand was on the bedroom door knob, he was shaking, his hand, that he had no control over, slowly pushed open the door and flipped on the light.

Cary lay on the bed; the color had drained from her naked body. The walls were red with her blood.

Red. Red. Red. Red everywhere, he hated red.

"Oh no, oh God no it can't be. It's Christmas, the kids want—the kids, where are the kids?" He couldn't breathe, he couldn't feel. He whirled around, took three long strides and opened the other bedroom. Frankie Jr. was on the floor in his favorite pajamas, still clutching his pillow, blood everywhere.

"Shelly! Shelly!" he screamed, but no sounds came from his mouth.

He heard water running in the bathroom. There he found Shelly, her yellow ducky bobbing up and down just like it did every night at bath time. She had been drowned.

"This isn't real, this is just a nightmare, I'll wake up." Was he speaking out loud or was it just his thoughts screaming in his head?

His legs started to buckle beneath him and he saw his killers in a split second before the wire closed around his throat. The wire tightened, choking back the scream before it could form. Two minutes later, life left Frankie. He dropped beside the tub, near his precious daughter.

They immediately pulled his wallet from his pants, and found three one hundred dollar bills neatly folded. They took the red and green envelope from his pocket and smiled when they ripped it open—$2,000 in cash.

Then they ransacked the house; opening drawers and closets, leaving a trail of destruction. Last task was the Christmas tree. They ripped open several presents and, finding nothing of value, they threw the gutted packages into the far corner.

Only then, their business complete, did the three strangers walk out of the house and into the storm.

CHAPTER 2: Wednesday, November 3, 2010

By the time most people were opening their eyes, James Jenkins was a free man on a bus headed for a new life. The sun was just beginning to light up the eastern sky and the dampness of the early morning sent a chill through his body. He had boarded the bus unfettered, cut loose from his prior life. Every mile was a mile closer to a normal life.

Five years was a long time to be in prison. He wasn't a criminal; he just got caught up in some stupid prank. He was through with that life. Never again. Prison had taught him a valuable lesson he promised never to forget. The past was past, the future held the world if only he could make it work like that.

But his brother had written him off because of it. A brother he loved and needed. Frankie couldn't believe James had become such a loser. He said he wanted nothing to do with him; after all he had his family to consider.

Frankie was his older brother, but he was a little slow. Mama had worried about him his whole life. "Remember, Jimmy," she said before she died, "you are the smart one; take care of your brother, he needs you."

Those words had tormented James in prison and played over and over in his mind.

Mama had great expectations for Frankie when he was born. His father wasn't so sure. It wasn't long before Effie Jenkins knew the truth about her beautiful baby son. By this time she was pregnant again. Being Hank's wife took a toll on a woman. After the doctor told her little Frankie wasn't retarded, but would probably be a little slower than other kids, Hank left them. It was the best thing that could have happened to her.

Three months later another son was born and Effie named him after James in the Bible. Her favorite verse was from James, chapter 1 verse 17. "Every good and perfect gift is from above and cometh down from the Father."

Mama died the year James graduated from high school. Her death changed everything. Frankie went to work at the local hardware store. One day the cutest girl he had ever seen came in. After that they were together all the time. When Frankie married Cary and went his own way, a burden was lifted from James's shoulders. He no longer heard Mama's voice in his head. He was free at last.

James had a few jobs but couldn't stay with anything. He found new friends who were wild and unsettled. When they started talking about holding up a gas station, he thought they were just kidding. Riding around in an old gray Pontiac, they stopped at Speedway and it still didn't sink in. It only took about five days for the law to catch up to them.

There had been a string of armed robberies in the county, and the judge wanted to make an example of James and his friends. James drew the maximum sentence, which meant he'd have to serve at least five years in prison before becoming eligible for parole. The only thing worse than the sentencing hearing that day was the bus ride to prison. He remembered thinking about how he had started out joyriding and wound up taking the worst ride of his life.

Florida State Prison was not a house of corrections; it was a college of higher learning. Convicts taught criminals new ways to lie, steal, cheat, even murder. What a man learned in prison, if he were so inclined, would secure his place in the criminal world.

With his brown hair cut short and clear blue eyes, James Jenkins was handsome beneath his fading prison pallor. But good looks were no asset in prison unless you could defend yourself. At thirty-two years old and five-ten, James had the physique of a man who worked out every day.

He made himself strong because the consequences of weakness behind bars weren't pretty. James also kept himself out of trouble. He was soon assigned a work duty, and earned access to the weight room.

Prison was a place for thinking. There wasn't a lot they allowed you to do there. They told you when to eat, when to shower, which wasn't often, and when to talk and when to shut up. Not much good can be said about prison. But when they're through with you, they give you a bus ticket and some clothes. He had earned his. And he promised himself every night that he would never go back.

Coming to Citrus City was a last-minute decision. The superintendent insisted he name a location. The superintendent had not received a confirmation letter from Frank, but he said a parole officer would contact James to confirm his whereabouts.

Now that he was a free man, he was going to start over. One of the most important things to him was the reference letter in the pocket of his cheap blue button-down shirt. With a job would come a gradual healing of the scars left by prison. He took out the letter and read it again, folded it, and returned it to his pocket.

Insecurity was his worst enemy. Each passing town frightened him. Inside, James was a scared little boy still hoping to become the man his mama envisioned. Outside, he was a guy who had spent five years being told exactly what to do every day. He was closer to being on his own than he could imagine.

In three weeks it would be Thanksgiving. James pulled out a photo from when he was a boy, of his family sitting in front of a table loaded with turkey and all the trimmings. He rehearsed what he would say to his brother. Frankie, five Thanksgivings without family was long enough, Mama would want us together, he would say.

The Trailways bus finally stopped at the depot in Citrus City. They called it a depot, but it was just a couple of extra chairs near the counter of the Second Street 7-11.

"Citrus City, all off for Citrus City," the bored driver brayed. It was James's stop, but he could hardly stand. He grabbed onto the seat in front of him. Am I having a heart attack? Will I survive long enough to step off the bus? The mid-morning sun drenched the streets but James hardly noticed. Why am I here? This was a big mistake. He felt a panic attack coming.

"You all right?" the driver asked.

"Yeah sir, I'm OK," James muttered.

But he wasn't, not at all. Take a deep breath, he said to himself. Several people got off, and he followed them. He looked around, but since no one was expecting him, no one was waiting for him. As he took his first step as a free man in Citrus City, a large black cat ran right between his legs.

"What the—" he was startled. The cat didn't stop but jumped right on the bus.

"Hey, get that damn cat off my bus!" the driver yelled. James laughed.

"OK, I'll get him, but it's not my cat. I just seem to attract bad luck."

"Coulda been worse," the driver said. "He coulda crossed your path."

James climbed back in the bus and began looking under the seats. He soon found the cat, which purred and brushed his black face against James's cheeks.

"If I had a place to stay I'd keep you," James said. "I guess we're both strays." He carried the cat off the bus, then shooed it down the street.

Citrus City was a town that realtors called typical old Florida. Downtown was three square blocks and boasted the 7-11, a small restaurant, and a dollar store. A few other buildings housed offices, a county building held the sheriff's office and the jail, just north of that was a used car lot. The liquor store wasn't far from the gas station, but the grocery store had closed long ago; all that remained was an empty store front.

"OK, I've come this far, I can make it," he said out loud. "But first I need wheels." He was thankful to have a starting point. The car dealer was a distant relative of Superintendent Peter Graham.

James had been a model prisoner and as such had caught the eye of the superintendent. Graham recognized the potential in James and suspected he had gotten a raw deal in court. Graham assigned him to work details that paid money to prisoners' accounts, so when James was released he had a small nest egg. Along with his money, he had the letter, addressed to Shorty's Used Cars in Citrus City. The letter was a character reference from the superintendent that he could use to help get a vehicle. The rest was up to him.

Shorty's Used Cars wasn't far from the depot. In fact, nothing was far from the depot. But the three-block walk took James almost half an hour. He pretended to look in the windows, but actually he was trying to get himself under control. Finally he was ready. He was glad to be here, he was adjusting with each minute. Head held high, shoulders back; he would make the change from prisoner to private citizen if it killed him. Mama could be proud of him after all.

At Shorty's he went directly to the office, not even stopping to check out the inventory. He wanted to be sure the letter was good before he got his hopes up. Years in prison does that to a man's confidence.

Shorty wasn't short at all, in fact, he was at least six feet tall and weighed about two hundred pounds; he was wearing Levis and a red plaid shirt. He looked to be about 55 or 56 years old and what little hair he had had probably been red. He was smiling and looked like an honest businessman.

James liked him immediately and stuck out his hand. "My name is James Jenkins, I need a car," he said cautiously. "I don't have a job yet, but expect to find one very soon. I have a letter from Peter Graham; I believe he is a relative of yours."

With this he handed the envelope to Shorty. The salesman opened and read it, and then he gave James the once-over. His heart started pounding; this was it. Would he get a break or would he be tripped up by his history? Then Shorty smiled.

"Where you been boy? I was expecting you last week. I got a call from Pete and he said someone would be stopping by and I should treat them right. That must be you."

Shorty's wide grin showed even white teeth. It belied a buoyant personality that had earned him "Business Man of the Year" several years in a row, according to the framed awards displayed prominently on his wall.

"Yeah, Pete is a good guy. Let's see what I can fix ya up with." He soon sold James on a four-door, dark green Ford. It was only four years old and had less than 60,000 miles.

"It belonged to a little old lady from Miami," Shorty laughed. James laughed too. He was sure Shorty used the line with everyone. It didn't take nearly as long to select a car as it did to complete the paper work. James had never owned a car before. This would be the start of a better life for him. Now he was ready to find his brother, Frankie.

From the car lot, James drove directly south toward old River Road. Sitting in his very own car made him feel like a million bucks. The sun was glaring in his eyes; he put the visor down and knew sunglasses would be a necessity.

The last time he talked to his brother, before the prison stay, Frankie said that he had found a good job at a big ranch on the edge of Citrus City. The town was small but he had a good sense of direction; he was sure he could find the place. He knew it was the only house on River Road, but maybe by now it was one of many.

The road sign was faded, bent, and almost useless. The road itself was overgrown with weeds and looked as if it hadn't seen much traffic lately. Pulling onto the road, he remembered from Frankie's description that it was only a mile off US 41. He had never been there and didn't know what to expect. But he turned left anyway, and hoped it got better. It didn't.

"I guess he's still the only house on this road," James said, and laughed out loud. The yard was just barely a clearing in the woods; high weeds and grass covered what appeared to have been a path to the sagging front porch. The windows were boarded up with warped plywood that looked as if it had been there for a while.

"Where is my brother?" James asked out loud. "Where are Cary and the kids?" Something in the shed caught his eye. He edged his way through an opening, risking injury and hoping the building wouldn't cave in on him. Leaning in a corner of the broken-down shed was a fishing rod, like the one he had given Frankie the last time they were together. After James wiped some of the dirt and grime from the handle with a handkerchief, he could make out initials: FJ. Why would Frankie leave his rod? It seemed to be in pretty good shape.

Walking back to the front of the house, he finished cleaning the rod as best he could, then put it in his car trunk. His failure to find his brother was just a minor delay. He would just go to town and ask around to find out where they had moved. After all, it was a small town. Everyone knew everyone else's business.

Shorty acted like he was friends with everyone; he'd know where Frankie was living. The used car salesman was surprised to see him back so soon.

"That car running like a charm, ain't she?" he asked.

"Hi Shorty, um, yes, the car's fine," James said. "I hate to make a pest of myself, but could you tell me the best way to find someone in this town?"

"You've come to the right place," Shorty boasted. "I've got connections and can probably find anyone in the entire state. Who's missing?"

"My brother was living around here but I guess he's moved. I can't seem to find him now."

"What's his name and last known address?" All business now, Shorty moved toward his desk and put his hands on the keyboard of his laptop.

"His name is Frank Jenkins; he lived just off River Road with his wife Cary." Shorty jerked his hands away from the keyboard and looked at James as if he had seen a ghost.

"Sit down, uh, have something to drink; I have to make a call," he stammered as he disappeared through a door marked PRIVATE. James was left to wonder what was going on. He began to get a knot in the pit of his stomach. Something wasn't right. He paced back and forth in a small space. Shorty returned a few minutes later, looking very serious.

"What's going on?" James asked. "What's the problem, can you help me or not?" James suddenly heard a jingling noise, turned, and saw Sheriff Doug Long walk through the door. His heart sank. *Are they sending me back already? What did I do?*

The sheriff was not as tall as Shorty but had 50 or 60 pounds on him. His uniform could have been a size larger and still would have been tight. He had his hat in one hand and a big white handkerchief in the other. His thinning hair was light brown and he had a problem keeping it plastered to his head. But he certainly was the law.

James felt like bolting out the door and probably would have, except the sheriff's bulk blocked the way out.

"Will someone please tell me what's going on?" he asked. He looked from Shorty to the sheriff, while fighting to control the sudden terror he felt.

"James, this is Sheriff Long. Sheriff, James Jenkins," Shorty said. He then stepped quickly out of the way. It wasn't his job anymore.

The sheriff held out his hand and James shook it, his hand was trembling. The sheriff's face was red and sweat was forming on his forehead. The last thing Sheriff Long wanted to do was to dredge up the worst day of his career.

"James, I'm afraid I have bad news for you," he said, wiping his forehead with the handkerchief. "Your family is gone—all of them."

"Gone where? What do you mean, they moved?" James asked.

"No, boy, they were killed—murdered."

James's knees buckled under him, he had to sit.

"What do you mean, murdered? When? Where? Who did it?"

"Murdered, right there on the ranch. Worst crime scene I ever saw. Even that sweet little girl, she was drowned," the sheriff was visibly shaken himself. "Who would do that to a little girl? Who would do that to any of them?" His mind recalled the gruesome details as if the murders had happened yesterday.

Shorty handed him a cup of water. James drank it, put his head in his hands and cried. After a short pause, Shorty handed him a paper towel.

"We worked day and night on this, nothing turned up," the sheriff said. "We think it was robbery because Frankie had just picked up his Christmas bonus from his boss; it was missing. There was a lot of speculation; one was that Cary might have had a jealous boyfriend on the side—sorry. We interrogated every suspicious person within miles, and every male that ever made a move on Cary, and there were a lot—she was a looker," the sheriff said. He paused. "Never was able to prove any of that. The case has been cold for some time now."

"You mean you never caught anyone?" James asked, looking from the sheriff to Shorty.

"No," the sheriff answered. "We had so little evidence, nothing to work with. There were no fingerprints. No forced entry, Cary must have let them in, which led us to believe she knew them. We don't even have a clue how many there were. We think it was more than one, just because of the damage."

James was at a loss for words. Frankie, Frankie, I'm so sorry.

"Let me say again, how sorry I am for your loss, if you stop by the office I will give you any personal items I have that belonged to the Jenkins," the sheriff mumbled.

The shock of hearing about his family was bad enough. But to know that no one had been charged and no one was actively working on the case was more than James could take. Why was he never notified? No suspects! No one working on the case? No way was he going to accept this!

* * *

The trip to the sheriff's office to collect Frankie's personal items took its toll. James knew he needed to find a bed for the night. Shorty suggested Days Inn, the only motel within miles. It was also clean and owned by, no surprise, someone Shorty knew.

James drove to the motel in a daze, and registered as if sleepwalking. His head could not quit spinning.

"A shower will help clear my mind," he said. Unbuttoning his shirt, he threw it as hard as he could at the bed; the rest of his clothes fell to the floor at his feet. Turning the shower on hot, he let it run until it was steaming. He stepped in and let the water wash over his entire body until he calmed down. He wasn't used to hot showers and he sure wasn't used to long showers; a man could get hurt in the shower where he came from.

He didn't even know how long he stood there. He only knew that when he turned off the faucet and stepped out on the bath mat, his head was a bit clearer. Life was taking him on yet another detour.

He turned on the television. Channel Five was showing a human interest story about a family who had lost everything in a fire. At the end of the segment an appeal was made for donations and information concerning the fire as a contact number flashed across the screen. James grabbed a pencil and scribbled down the number on a pad of paper he found by the phone.

"Maybe I can get some help from this station," he told the television.

CHAPTER 3: Thursday, November 4

Athena Sands eased out of bed and stretched. She walked out on the balcony of the guest bedroom. The blonde streaks glinted in her thick auburn hair as she pushed it back from her eyes. She opened her arms to the bright orange glow rising over the pine trees. Their smell tickled her nose like a can of cola held too close to her nose.

Yesterday she had escaped an unusually cold early November in Chicago. Today, she embraced the sun of Citrus City. She wanted to absorb all the rays to carry back to the cold, dark Windy City that she called home.

Fragrant honeysuckle and blue morning glories covered the rustic fence that separated the back yard from the beginning of the woods. She truly was in paradise. It brought back memories of when she was much younger. Athena was born in Florida and now lived in Chicago, a beautiful city she loved. But she still missed home.

Athena was glad her younger sister had invited her to stay through Thanksgiving, although she knew the visit wasn't a pleasure trip. Beth needed help coping with the death of her husband, a sheriff's deputy who had died in a car crash six months ago.

The aroma drifting upstairs brought her back to reality; her sister was awake. Turning slowly, allowing the warmth to soak every inch of her body, she stepped back into the bedroom, donned her robe and headed for the kitchen downstairs.

"Good morning, Athena," Beth said "Did you sleep OK last night?"

"Better than OK; I haven't slept that sound in months," she answered honestly. "The view out over the woods is wonderful and you even have sunshine for me. You can't imagine how cold it was at home yesterday. I'm glad I'm here."

With its granite counters and ivory colored cabinets, the kitchen was a welcome spot to sit and chat, a secret most women discovered early in life. Beth and Athena didn't always see eye to eye. Beth's whole life revolved around her children now that her husband was gone. Athena, on the other hand, was a hard-charging businesswoman running a publishing house in Chicago. Her profession was her family. But the sisters had sat in kitchens many a day and talked until their differences seemed to melt away.

As Beth poured the coffee, Athena set the table. Beth's children made their way to the kitchen. Taylor, a junior at Sherman High School, had brown hair that topped a six-foot frame. He looked so much like his father it was uncanny. Missy, a freshman, was a blond, five-foot-two bundle of energy.

"Mom," Taylor mumbled with his mouth full of toast. "I need twenty bucks. We have to pay for our football banquet tickets today. Hey, Aunt Athena, my new coach is a real hunk, let me introduce you," Taylor added.

Athena looked at Beth and then back to Taylor.

"I still remember the last hunk you introduced me to, no thanks," Athena laughed. Last time she was here it was his biology teacher, a great-looking guy who would rather cut up frogs than go out to dinner. Not her idea of a hunk.

Beth made a face at her daughter. "Missy, you have to eat, I made you a piece of toast and juice, and you can't leave without eating something."

Missy made a face right back, but she downed the juice and took the toast with her. Taylor took the money Beth was holding and both kids disappeared out the door. As soon as the door slammed things got quiet. Athena knew Beth wasn't ready to talk about her loss, so she had planned a shopping day that would please them both.

In no time, working together, the two women had cleared the table, washed the breakfast dishes, and hit the road. They had decided on the mall in the next town over, Vista. Their first stop was a shop carrying major league apparel. Athena picked up a Chicago Bears sweatshirt for Taylor.

"I'll make a Bears fan out of him yet," she said. "You can't blame an aunt for trying."

Beth laughed, but Athena could tell her mind was somewhere else. Athena shrugged her shoulders. She seldom allowed herself the luxury of a relaxed shopping excursion, so she decided to just enjoy herself. Beth would talk when she was ready.

They shopped until noon, then the food court called their names. Finding a table wasn't a problem, it seemed the major population of snowbirds hadn't flown in yet.

"Let's take a look at the new book store," Athena said as she nodded toward Barbara's Book Depot. "I have to mix a little business with pleasure." She loved books and it gave her a chance to mix a little business with this outing.

Robert Louis Sands, her father-in-law, had founded Sands Publishing Company of Chicago, the company his son John inherited. Athena was a struggling writer when she met John. Their courtship was a page right out of a fairy tale, maybe *Cinderella*. Prince Charming never lost his charm and Cinderella proved to be as exciting as anyone he had ever met.

They married and the business thrived. Marriage improved both of them—until the windy evening John died of a heart attack. Six years together seemed like the blink of an eye. She lost the desire to work or write. It took two years for her to accept the fact that John wasn't coming home.

Running a business was a difficult job. But one morning she woke up after dreaming of her late husband, and knew she had to snap out of it. John would have wanted her to go on. She began to write again, paid attention to the business, and soon Sands Publishing was thriving again.

Athena developed a sixth sense for the written word; she was able to spot a future best seller after reading the first draft of a manuscript. But she remained a very hands-on professional, leading by example as her children's books constantly sold well.

Entering Barbara's Book Depot, the first thing that grabbed Athena's attention was the marvelous aroma of coffee coming from the little café tucked in the corner. Customers were reading quietly to themselves, each lost in their own worlds. Athena was thrilled when she saw people reading, it was almost a lost art. With all the electronics, kids would rather watch a video or play a game on their i-whatever.

The children's section had five books published by Sands Publishing; she was elated. A few aisles away, she gravitated to the mysteries. Children's books were her love, her bread and butter, but mysteries intrigued her. She was pleasantly surprised by the number of new women authors whose books she discovered.

Selecting one, she went searching for Beth, and found her in the cookbook section. Athena's mouth watered. A new cookbook meant something great for dinner tonight.

They browsed for a while and finally left the mall. The day had been a success; if all they had wanted to do was shop. But Athena suspected Beth needed the downtime and the company more than the shopping.

The new recipe was a success, and after dinner the kids retired to their respective study areas. Athena and Beth cleaned the kitchen and reflected on their day. Later, homework done, Missy and Taylor said goodnight.

Taking glasses of iced tea, the two women kicked off their shoes and moved to the family room. It was time for the news and weather on television. While national news spread the usual doom and gloom, the local situation was much lighter. With only three weeks until Thanksgiving, tourists were just beginning to flock to beaches. Local businesses were feeling better about the prospects of the holiday season.

But then a different type of local news story came over the air.

"James Jenkins, thirty-two, just recently released from Florida State Prison, is in Citrus City and asking anyone with information about his brother, Frank Jenkins, to contact him through a post office box," said Rod Manly, the silver-haired, velvet-voiced announcer who usually did the human interest stories.

"Frank and his family were all murdered five years ago in Citrus City," Manly said. "James wasn't notified at the time and only found out yesterday when he arrived in town hoping to surprise his brother. He was devastated by the news. No one had been arrested in this homicide and the sheriff's department considers it a cold case. James vows he will not rest until he has answers to all his questions."

The story ended with a recap of the case and a contact number for viewers who may have information about the murders.

"Martin worked on that case," Beth said. "When he died, I thought I couldn't go on, but I knew I had to because of the kids. After a couple months I really thought I was going to be all right, but now I struggle to get through the day. I'm so glad you're here."

That revelation seemed to open a floodgate. She picked up a pillow and hugged it. "Will I ever feel good again? Will I be able to make it through a day without crying? Martin was a good man, a good husband and father. Why was he taken from us?"

Years ago, Athena might have urged Beth to buck up and get back to living. She would have told Beth her own story of overcoming the loss of her own husband. But she was older now, and understood that there were times when the best response was reassurance and support.

"You're doing fine; you can't expect to feel great all the time," she said softly. "Grieving is an emotional process, everyone does it at their own pace."

"I haven't even been able to go through Martin's things yet." Beth's voice was strained. "Before you go home, I need your help, please."

"Sure," Athena nodded as she pulled Beth close. "Whenever you're ready; I'm here for you."

CHAPTER 4: Friday, November 5

Just before heading to work, Sheriff Doug Long usually watched the morning news. That's how he learned about James Jenkins's plea for help.

"Oh my God, that boy went to the media!" Sheriff Long sputtered.

He immediately called Tom Wiley, who had been a deputy for about as long as the sheriff had been in office. Wiley was a hard worker who meant well, but never seemed to get the big picture. He hopped when the sheriff said jump, and usually did what he was told. After Martin's death he became Sheriff Long's right-hand man—until Keenan came on board.

"Tom, did you see the news? Channel Five?" Long shouted. "That Jenkins boy's asking for help in finding his brother's killer! This is a heads-up, get in early today and let's see what we can do to contain this."

Forty-five minutes later, Tom Wiley arrived in the office. Long was rapidly pacing, sweat already visible on his forehead, when Wiley entered. He started talking before Wiley could even say hey.

"We'll meet this head on, with a press conference of our own," Long barked. "I've called the mayor and that TV reporter. But first let's get our stories in sync. Where's McDuff? I want him here. He looks good on TV." Long tried to laugh.

Keenan walked in the door, surprised to see Sheriff Long so animated. He looked at his watch; same time he usually showed up. Deputy Wiley was in early, not as wild-eyed as the sheriff, but caught up in conversation with him.

"What's up, guys?" he said.

"It looks like that Jenkins boy went to the media with his case. So I've decided to call a press conference myself and let the public know we didn't have a snowball's chance in hell of solving that case. We still don't. Case closed!"

"Wait a minute, Sheriff," Keenan interrupted. "What Jenkins boy, what case?" Long explained his encounter with James. Keenan was surprised that he was the last to hear this, but he wasn't surprised at the sheriff's reaction.

"We can reopen this case," he said. "It's done all the time. With new technology we might get lucky."

"We worked hard on that case," Long shot back. "Some cases are never solved; this will be one of them." Long's face was red and he was mad. "We may not be as educated as you, but let me tell you; Martin was here and we had detectives from Ocean Park here too. There wasn't anything to work with."

Long look at Tom for a little back up. "What do you think?"

"Well, Sheriff, I was here when it happened and I know how hard we worked on it," Tom answered. "We didn't have much evidence. I know how hard Martin worked on it; it couldn't be done."

Wiley wasn't an investigator, Keenan thought, but he was a first class ass kisser. He fit right in here.

"Sheriff, let me ask you something," Keenan said. "When do you expect to have this, this press conference?"

"I've already called the mayor and the TV reporter. They will be here soon. Make sure your uniform is clean and your hair is combed. I'll do all the talking; you and Wiley just stand there and look intelligent." He smirked. "That won't be too hard, will it?"

"Are you calling James Jenkins?" Keenan asked, ignoring Long's jab.

"No, not yet. After the press conference, if he hasn't gone away we'll have to do something. Now, both of you had better prepare yourselves for the gentlemen of the press."

As if on cue, the TV van pulled up in front of the office; attracting the attention of diners at the café next door. They came out on the sidewalk to see what was going on.

"Set up right over there, boys," the sheriff said grandly as the TV news crew entered. "Anybody want a coffee? Wiley, take some orders and go next door for some donuts and stuff."

"No thanks, Sheriff," said Rod Manly, the silver-haired announcer who had broken the Jenkins story.

"I'll take care of you, boss," said Lola, the frisky waitress from the café, pushing her way through the knot of people who had followed her over from next door. "You boys want a little sugar?" she asked, sidling up to Rod. "My, that silver does become you," she said reaching up and patting the announcer's hair.

"Well, now that you mention it, Miss—" Manly said in his deepest newsman voice.

"Oooh, that voice of yours," Lola squealed. "I'd like to add a little cream to that coffee!"

"Hey, hey!" Sheriff Long shouted. "Lola, you make eyes at your customers on your own time, I've got an office to run. Wiley, clear these people out of here."

As Wiley jumped to comply with Long's orders, Manly adroitly separated himself from Lola.

"Harrumph," said Manly, straightening his tie and signaling to the cameraman. "Let's ask the sheriff a few questions."

The sheriff sat at his desk, slicked back his hair, and motioned for the two deputies to stand behind him. Flanked by his men, Sheriff Long smiled. Manly looked toward the cameraman, who gave a thumbs up. The red light gleamed as he went to work.

"We're here with Sheriff Douglas Long, Citrus City's top cop, regarding an unsolved murder that happened right here, five years ago," Manly crooned. "As you know from last night's broadcast, ranch hand Frank Jenkins, his wife, and two small children were killed in cold blood during the Christmas season here. The case remains unsolved."

The sheriff grimaced at Manly's last line, but then turned on a broad campaign smile as the announcer turned to question him.

"What have you done to solve this case?" Manly asked the sheriff. "Why have the killers gone unpunished for so long?"

"Um, no murder case is ever closed until it is solved," the sheriff said. "And we discovered a relative who claims he may have information about this case that could help us solve it."

"Would that be James Jenkins, the brother of the deceased?" Manly asked.

"I'm sorry, Mr. uh, Mr. Man," the sheriff said huffily, "but I'd rather not comment on an ongoing investigation."

"So the investigation has been re-opened?" Manly fired back. "Oh, and the name's Manly."

"I repeat, I'd rather not comment on an ongoing investigation."

Once those words left Sheriff Long's mouth, he knew he had been tricked. "OK, this press conference is over," he snapped, rising from his chair and ripping off the lapel mike a technician had clipped to his shirt.

Keenan barely held back a laugh.

"But sheriff, one more question; where is Mr. Jenkins, the brother of the deceased? Have you talked to him?"

"I said no more questions."

The filming was over. Moments later, Sheriff Long stood there watching the media van drive off into the morning sunshine. When it was out of sight he turned and entered the office.

"Uh, I'm going next door for a cup of coffee," Keenan said. He knew the sheriff felt bad, and didn't want to be around the man in a mood.

"Wait a minute, Keenan," the sheriff said. He took a seat at his desk, sighed, and glanced over at Keenan and Tom. "That didn't turn out the way I expected."

Shit, thought Sheriff Long. A man's family was gone, he needed help, answers, closure. And now, because I shot off my mouth for that smart-ass news guy, I have to get back into this case.

"I just opened an investigation I said was closed. Keenan, call Jenkins, I know where he's staying, and set up an appointment for an interview. Wiley you need to get back on patrol, I'll call you if I need you, see you at five."

Tom put his hat on and headed out.

Sheriff Long went into the conference room to retrieve the Jenkins files from the cold case drawer. He pulled the evidence boxes from the shelf and lined them up on the table. Then he sat there and stared at the files. Was the answer here? Could they find an answer? Where to start? He began to read. Times like these were when he really missed Martin. His late deputy was a detail-oriented investigator. He, on the other hand, was a delegator who allowed Martin or Tom Wiley to handle everything.

I'm losing touch, he thought, I'm losing the fire to fulfill the duties of the office. Is it time to step down? If I don't handle it right, this case could be my swan song. Then my biggest worry would be finding the best fishing spot every day. Was that what I want? Now that Martin was gone, maybe that know-it-all Keenan could step in. Lord knows, Wiley doesn't have the brains for anything more than directing traffic.

As if on cue, Keenan stepped into the conference room. And then Sheriff Long said something he had never said before.

"Keenan, come over here, we've got work to do."

Keenan was the newest deputy in the office. He had been hired after the accidental death of Deputy Martin Filmore six months ago. He lived nearby and had been commuting to Tampa, where he worked for the Hillsboro Sheriff's Office as an investigator. That commute had been wearing on him and he had welcomed the chance to work closer to home. But the grass isn't always greener on the other side—or in this case, closer to home. In Tampa something was happening daily. Here every day was just like the day before. Sheriff Long drove him crazy with his uneducated, unsophisticated, unprofessional ways.

"What's up?"

Long looked tired. "Keenan what's your take on this Jenkins case?"

"Winston Churchill once said, 'The farther backward you look, the farther forward you are likely to see.'"

"What are you talking about, who the hell is Winston Churchill?" The sheriff was still on a short fuse. That TV reporter had embarrassed him in front of everybody. "And what do I care what he says?"

"What I mean is, maybe we have to go back farther than five years to solve this."

Keenan's red hair was starting to curl up around his ears but it wasn't unruly. Freckles on his face seemed to dance around his blue eyes. Sheriff Long ran the Keenan file through his mind as he eyed the younger man. He knew Keenan played guitar and sang at the local dive, Captain Kidd's, when he wasn't on duty. He knew he was married with one son. And he knew that maybe he had found the perfect fall guy for the cold case.

"OK, Keenan, you're on it," the sheriff said. Who knows, maybe the new guy could turn up something new. If not, he'd put the blame on the young know-it-all.

Keenan had never worked a cold case and this would be a test. "I think you better call James; we can go from there," Keenan answered.

The sheriff tossed the Jenkins file in front of Keenan. "We'll call him," he said. "But first, read this file, then I'll fill you in and you can give me your take on the whole thing."

It didn't take Keenan long to read everything they had on the case because there wasn't a lot of information. It was in a single file folder; for four deaths there were photos, autopsy reports, written interviews and a few departmental notes. He was surprised, he had expected much more.

He was starting to formulate a plan: start from scratch; time consuming but their best bet, considering what there was to work with.

"Well, there isn't a lot here. Whatever happened to Jake Wells? We will need to find him." He looked at Long and saw confusion on his face. Long was sweating hard. Maybe having to work is new to him, Keenan thought.

"He's moved, but I know where he keeps himself," the sheriff said as he reached in his pocket for his handkerchief. "I remember he really took it hard, Frankie was his best friend."

Keenan nodded "Everything pointed to a senseless killing," he said. "Why would someone kill Frankie Jenkins and his family, just to rob his house and steal his Christmas bonus?"

He re-read the file. According to witnesses, Jenkins wasn't the brightest person around but he was undoubtedly the friendliest. Never a run-in with the law and never had trouble with anyone that could be verified. He lived out on "God's little acre" probably the only person for miles who could live so isolated.

Cleveland Parnell, Frankie's employer, said he was a good employee who always did his job, never asked for a raise, and never questioned authority. He was just that rare man who was content to be where he was. The family was usually seen together, except when he was fishing—apparently Frankie loved to fish.

"Here is the rest of it, there's very little." The sheriff pushed the two boxes toward him, ashamed at the pathetic amount of evidence. "Case #39005" in bold black letters identified the boxes containing all they had in physical evidence. Long mopped his face with his handkerchief. He sensed Keenan's critical eyes on him.

"Oh, I said I would call that Jenkins boy," he said breaking the tension. "You mind sitting in on the interview?"

"Well, it's my case now, right, sheriff?" Keenan answered.

The sheriff grunted.

"Well, let's get him in here," Keenan said. "I think we need to start from scratch. We can set up interviews with everyone again, including Cleveland Parnell—that's the guy who owns the ranch where Jenkins worked, right?"

"Whoa," Sheriff Long reached in his pocket again for his handkerchief. "He isn't going to like this, so let's get all our ducks in a row before we call him. I'd rather stick bamboo shoots under my fingernails than upset Parnell. Hunh, he'll probably stick them under my nails himself." He laughed at his own joke, and then remembered himself. "We'll start with the Jenkins boy; go ahead, you give him a call."

* * *

James was surprised by Deputy McDuff's call, and eagerly agreed to see him. In his excitement, he got ready too early. So he sat in his motel room, thinking and killing time until his appointment. He was having a hard time digesting all he had heard in the last two days. The room was bright, the sun shone through the open windows. He pulled back the curtains and lay back on the bed. He looked at the clock, closed his eyes and thought of a much happier, less stressful time.

"Oh Frankie, I'm so sorry. I'll make it up to you," hammered like a broken record in his head.

When James opened his eyes, his face was wet and red; he had been crying. He remembered his dream, he and Frankie, headed down to the fishing spot behind their home. But that was gone, all gone. He'd never fish with Frankie again. But maybe he could do something to make up for failing him. Maybe he could help give Frankie's soul some peace by finding whoever laid him and his family in their graves.

He had just enough time to get himself together before the meeting with the sheriff. He washed his face and walked out the door. The Days Inn was just a few miles north of town and the ride didn't take long.

He never thought he would enter a law enforcement office willingly again. He hated the thought of being there; too many bad experiences. But there he was. He barely remembered it from the day when he picked up Frankie's personal things. That day was still a fog in his mind. Today it looked even smaller. There were three desks, with hard chairs that had seen a lot of wear. Each desk had a nameplate on it, but there were few personal items giving clues as to the lives of the occupants. On the wall were old and new wanted posters. As he started to sit he heard voices coming from a room in the back.

The sheriff called out to him to come in. He walked into the dull gray conference room, with its naked bulb hanging from the overhead fixture. Bars on the single window would make it hard to escape. He was sure the state had a blueprint for these rooms and every sheriff's office had one. They all looked alike. Not that he had seen many, but he had seen enough and they scared him.

"James, meet Keenan McDuff, my deputy." The men shook hands and James took a seat. Keenan saw a scared young man. He had already checked his record in the data base: First offense, long sentence.

"James I think you should know we held a press conference that will be on the news soon. You created quite a stir with your little TV appearance and we were forced to respond," the sheriff said, looking sideways at James to gauge his reactions.

"It's OK though," Keenan chimed in, "we'll get through it. But, please, don't do it again, unless you talk to us first. We're here to help you."

We'll get through it? James thought. What about Frankie, his wife, his kids, they didn't get through it. Who are these people? What have they done for my brother but lie and drag their feet? But he kept his composure. Maybe they were ready to try again.

"Could you tell me how you expect to solve this? Can I help?" James hadn't heard anything encouraging yet. But he was trying to keep a positive attitude; it was very hard. Right now his insides boiled.

"We intend to re-interview Jake Wells, he was Frank's best friend," Keenan said. "Also, Cleveland Parnell, Frank's employer, has agreed to talk to us tomorrow. We're preparing a new list of questions for both men."

The sheriff spoke up. "We'll get a handle on this."

"What can I do?" James asked. "I need to be involved, I need to help. I'll do anything, put up posters, go back on TV, anything, please."

"Don't do anything yet," Sheriff Long snapped. You've done enough already, he thought, I just hope you can keep your mouth shut in the future.

For the next two hours they read the notes, looked at evidence and kicked around theories. Nothing new had been received since the broadcast, but there was still hope. James left with the promise from the sheriff that he would call him within a few days, as soon as he had time to organize the files again. Sheriff Long promised to keep him in the loop on everything they could.

When he left the parking lot he drove around town to become more familiar with it. This town was bigger than he first thought. He had already gone south to the ranch and north to the hotel; now he would try east and west to get the lay of the land before going back to his room.

*　*　*

At the end of the day, when both deputies had gone, Sheriff Long leaned back in his chair, closed his eyes and tried to clear his mind.

"What have I missed?"

He straightened up, and knew it was a time of resolution. He must use long-forgotten skills, skills he was sure had existed at one time. He had to work for a change. He stood and began to pace; he thought better on his feet. Keenan was younger, educated and would be an asset. He was cocky and too uptight; but he seemed to have the right attitude to work this case. Maybe with a little luck they could develop some leads. Otherwise, it was back to the cold case file.

CHAPTER 5: Saturday, November 6

The sun rose, bright and golden; no clouds in the sky. It was a little cooler than yesterday, but even in Florida it gets cooler in November. The kids had left for the homecoming game pep rally, so the sisters had the house to themselves. Athena wanted Beth to feel better. She wanted her to start to live again. So cleaning out Martin's closets and his personal office was the job of the day.

"One more cup of coffee and we are ready," Beth said. Martin's office was large and if she could force herself to walk up the stairs she would convert it to a useful space again. But she really wasn't prepared to tackle what she called Phase One. The past was on her mind, this would be hard for her.

"If we start in Martin's office it might be easier on me," she said. "He kept a lot of files which he had been transferring to his computer; I hope to get rid of these ugly metal file cabinets. They cover too much wall space. It's a great room, but it needs a makeover."

Athena knew she would have to tread lightly with her; a little innocent conversation would help. "How long had Martin worked for the sheriff's department?"

"Fifteen years," Beth said.

"I wouldn't expect a lot of crime here," Athena said.

"Martin thought it was about as exciting as watching grass grow."

"How was Sheriff Long to work with?"

"He was a great delegator, he left everything to Martin. He knew where to fish or hunt, but the only time he stayed in the office was if he knew Cleveland Parnell was in town."

"Who's Parnell? And why would he hang around for him?"

"Mr. Parnell owns most of Citrus City, his family started here years ago." Beth sighed and stood up. "Let's get to it."

This room above the garage had been added a few years ago and designed as Martin's office. It was built with a balcony, which greatly improved the ambience.

It would make a great media room or a room for entertaining.

Furnished with a leather sofa and masculine décor, it was definitely a man's space. Two Lazy Boy recliners were positioned in front of a flat-screen television mounted on the wall. It was also a dad's place. Trophies and medals won by his children filled the glass case against the north wall. The kids had to be proud of the way their dad displayed everything they had ever won, from first grade and Little League to high school football and cheerleading. Pictures were on every surface, Missy and Taylor were shown growing up before your eyes. Situated on the desk were a computer, a laser printer, and a picture of Beth.

The morning light flooded through the floor-to-ceiling windows. The natural illumination left no room for the sad reflections filling Beth's mind. But still, she looked around and her eyes misted over.

"I haven't been able to come in this room since—well, I really haven't been up here since Martin died," she said. "I should dust and vacuum, but first let's get these files out of here; they seem to be stacked everywhere. Doug Long can pick them up and do whatever he wants with them. Then we can get rid of these file cabinets. I'm sure Goodwill will take them."

Athena powered on the computer and the screen came to life. After a few clicks she could see what Martin was working on. His flash drive was still in the computer.

Beth flipped on the TV and walked over to the file cabinet, opening drawers.

"Do you think I should call Sheriff Long or wait until we pack this up and organize it? These are duplicates, I'm sure. They're all photocopies. I sure hope he knew that Martin had all this in his home office. I just want it gone."

"Why don't we leave them here for a while," Athena said. "I could get some real information here. Wow! You and I could collaborate on a book together, a murder mystery? I'm thinking we could find a lot of good ideas —"

"—Wait a minute." Beth cut her off. "I want these out of here, and I'm not writing a book with you. You do what you want, but leave me out. I'm throwing this stuff at Sheriff Long as soon as he gets over here."

Beth fumed as she moved to the only closet in the room. It contained a gun safe, Cabelo's Classic Series. Martin had paid a lot of money for it, but said it was worth every penny. It was 12-gauge two-piece plated construction and could withstand a house fire. It had an e-lock which he always kept secured.

"I hate these things," she said. She and Martin had spent more than one date at the practice range. Now marriage, motherhood, and maturity had changed her outlook about guns. She had no use for them. "I'm getting rid of all the guns too; I don't want them in the house." She opened the lock.

"There is a gun missing," she said, staring at the empty space where a firearm should have been. She made a note to ask the sheriff about it. Making sure to lock the safe, she closed the closet door. She would have Sheriff Long make a report on the missing gun.

Athena was busy herself, printing everything on the flash drive.

Beth crossed the room and stood staring out beyond the fence. The woods were quiet and still. That's the thing about life, she thought. Sometimes when you stand very still and watch you see the world the way it really is.

"Hey Beth, take a look at this," Athena broke the silence as she plucked a few sheets of paper from the print tray. "Can you at least take a glance? You were here, give me a clue. I'm using this in my book."

Beth took the sheets of paper and began reading. Her face blanched as she scanned her late husband's notes.

JENKINS CASE # BC 39005

Known facts: Date of Death - Dec. 15th, Time of Death 6- 12 PM

1. Frank Jenkins age 28 - strangled with a thin wire {?} body found in bathroom fully dressed in jeans and denim shirt, white and black Nikes covered with mud and water jeans pockets were turned inside out and wallet was empty on the floor near the door, Christmas card ripped open—contained

bonus from boss, $2000 cash--- autopsy report: strangulation. (make appointment with Parnell)

2. Cary Jenkins age 25 - throat cut, possible fillet knife {?} 9 stab wounds in upper torso, cuts on arms and hands, indicating struggle with attacker{s} body found in master bedroom nude -- autopsy report -- any of the three stab wounds to heart area could have caused death. No signs of sexual assault.

3. Frank Jr. age 5 - 3 stab wounds in upper torso, body found in children's bedroom, dressed in pajamas -- autopsy -- any of stab wounds could cause death

4. Shelly age 3- nude, drowned, body in bath tub

Arriving @ 6:00 a.m. Sheriff Long, deputies, Filmore and Wiley

Arriving @ 6:40 a.m. Photographer

Arriving @ 6:45 a.m. Ambulance

Arriving @ 7:15 a.m. Coroner

Discovered by Jake Wells. Jake Wells had an alibi, in Captain Kidd's Bar until 11:45 p.m. Dec. 15th. He told everyone he was going fishing the next day. His truck was packed with coolers and fishing gear.

Witnesses--- none

Weather conditions -- severe storms, starting about 7 p.m. Lasting about an hour to one and one-half hours then turning cooler.

"It looks like Martin was taking another look at this case." Athena said.

At that moment the TV caught their attention.

"The big story this week is the renewed interest in a five-year-old homicide in Citrus City," the announcer said. "Friday morning Sheriff Douglas Long held a press conference to announce that his department is taking a fresh look at the deaths of the Jenkins family. Frank and Cary Jenkins and their two young children were discovered murdered in their home five years ago. Robbery was the only motive established and no suspects were discovered. When asked why the sudden interest in the case, the sheriff replied, 'No murder case is ever closed until solved and we have discovered a relative who claims he may have some information about this case that could help us solve it.' That's all the sheriff would say, but sources close to that office tell us Frank Jenkins's brother showed up and was horrified to learn of the tragedy. He issued a public plea for help. If you have any information, contact the sheriff's office."

Both women were caught off guard. Athena reacted first, "Now that's more than a coincidence," she said. "He's talking about same crime Martin was working on in those notes."

But Beth had also seen the notes and she wasn't listening. She had that same far-away look Athena had noticed earlier in the morning. Then she moved purposefully to the phone without answering Athena. She picked up the phone and dialed, paused, then spoke. "Hello, this is Beth Filmore, I wonder if the sheriff is available?"

"What are you doing, Beth?" Athena asked.

"Shush," she hissed. "I'm making it go away."

"Sheriff? Yes, yes it's been hard, thank you, I miss him too," Beth said in response to the sheriff's awkward condolences. It had been months since the sheriff had checked in on her and the kids, she thought, as if Martin's death put an end to any concern the lawman might have had for the family.

Meanwhile, Athena continued rummaging through the files. She didn't know much about actual crime files, but the Jenkins file seemed too small. The files were from the flash drive that had been left in the computer. She removed the drive and put it in a metal box on the desk, which already held several other flash drives. They could check those later. The box originally held Altoids, Martin's favorite mints.

"Sheriff, we have some information about that murder that's been on TV, the one you had a press conference about," Beth said. "Yes, we found it on Martin's computer." Beth didn't want anyone, not even the sheriff, in her husband's office. She wanted all of the crime stuff out of there; the sooner the better. Athena could write her story in Chicago, for all she cared.

"Yes sir, Monday afternoon at 3, yes, we'll be there—thanks."

As she hung up the phone, Athena confronted her. "Beth, this is good stuff. Let's go through it first. You know the sheriff—"

"—Athena, I've had enough," Beth screamed. "First I had to bury my husband, now you come down here and want to dig him up again. I know you're all Miss Big City, with your frosted hair and Chicago ways, and we're just country bumpkins. But we're real people, not characters for some book you want to write. Stop making this into *Who Killed Roger Rabbit*. I want an end to this!"

With that, she turned and stormed down the stairs, leaving a chastened Athena to pick up the pieces.

CHAPTER 6: Monday, November 8

Three o'clock was an awkward hour for Beth and Athena to see the sheriff in his office. Beth had to deal with the kids coming home from school. Fortunately, Taylor had football practice. And Missy was only too happy to hang out at her girlfriend's house until Beth picked her up.

Beth had not been to the office in six months, so the apprehension she was feeling was very real. She remembered many lunches eaten in this room with Martin, just so they could have time together. She missed that. On the drive over she continued to second-guess herself. She wanted the police out of her life, but she didn't know if this was the way.

After perfunctory greetings, the sheriff poured coffee for them and led them into the conference room. The whiteboard was respectfully covered, with no signs of the brainstorming session the sheriff and Keenan went through earlier.

Beth remembered the long table, scarred from too many smokers in too many long discussions. Now the building was non-smoking, for which the women were grateful.

Evidence boxes and file folders lay scattered on the table. The sheriff had made an effort to stack things into somewhat neater piles. He turned the boxes around so the labels could only be seen from his side, hoping Beth and Athena wouldn't get a hard look at them. Beth was so focused on what she wanted from the sheriff that she failed to notice Athena eyeing all the boxes and files cluttering up this room.

The lone window let very little natural light in, and the chairs were not designed for comfort. Drab gray was the official wall color. They must have gotten a deal on the paint, Beth thought, each room was the same shade. It wasn't this miserable when Martin was here.

Sheriff Long didn't look very enthusiastic about the meeting, so Beth got right to the point. She had promised Athena she would. And she didn't want Athena causing a scene.

"Sheriff, was Martin working on a case when he died?"

If she had asked about her widow's benefits or the upcoming Neighborhood Taste of Citrus City, Sheriff Long would not have batted an eye. But he wasn't expecting her question; he couldn't recall Beth ever questioning anything and it shook him for a moment. He eyed her sister; she must be pumping Beth up. She sure didn't seem to be the wallflower her sister was.

"Martin wasn't working on a case, as far as I know, however, we both know he was like a dog with a bone about some things. Why do you ask?"

Athena couldn't keep silent any longer. "Shouldn't you know what's going on in your office?"

Long looked at her—nope, no wallflower.

"If he was working off the record, would he share it with you?" she prodded.

"Um, that is, we often talk theory or hypothetical cases, but when he was working on anything he usually let me know, out of courtesy to this office. Documentation was important and there were no open files in his desk when we cleared it out."

At this rate, they would be here all day, Athena thought, bantering back and forth. These small town people never seemed to get to the point. How could she move things along?

"The other day you announced you were reopening a five-year-old case. The day before that a man made an appeal on television for information concerning his brother. This is the same case, right?"

Sheriff Long was surprised by the question, and since the table was littered with the case files he knew he couldn't lie. She had seen the appeal on television, she saw his statement about reopening an old case, she knew this office would handle the local crime; what was her interest?

Keenan walked into the room. He had been listening from his desk, and knew Sheriff Long could use reinforcements. Keenan had mixed feelings about stepping into the middle of the discussion. It was funny watching the sheriff squirm, but he felt for the older man. Besides, there was professional pride at stake and Beth was a lawman's widow.

"I don't blame Mr. Jenkins, if it was my brother I would turn this town upside down looking for help," Keenan said.

Beth's mind churned. She began to have second thoughts about giving the sheriff what she had. She hesitated to bring up the files. Maybe she should just leave the sheriff and his office out of this and destroy them herself.

"Is there anything else I can do for you ladies?" Keenan asked with a smile.

For Beth this was the last straw, she resented being talked down to, and she disliked even worse being rushed out of the office. Keenan's attitude was all wrong, and the sheriff was doing little to stand up for her.

"Saturday, Athena and I started to clean Martin's office at home," Beth said, choosing her words carefully. "We found a file on the computer and a stack of file folders pertaining to Jenkins. It was so ironic, considering the news story and your announcement, that I wondered if you had had Martin checking out new leads or something."

"Martin worked for you, he was working on the Jenkins case, yet you said on television that it was a cold case," Athena said bluntly. "What's going on?"

"Actually, we hadn't talked about this case in a long time," Sheriff Long replied, looking at Keenan to bail him out. "I can't remember the last time it was mentioned. I know how close you and Martin were, if he had been on the case, I'm sure you would know it," he continued, since Keenan wasn't going to defuse the women. "But in light of all that's happened in the last two days I would like to see that information. I'm sure there's nothing new, but just the same, why don't I drop by and pick it up?"

Athena suspected he was dodging her questions as best he could.

"If Martin wasn't doing this officially, why is there all this secrecy?" Athena asked. "He didn't say anything to Beth or to you and yet the last file in his computer was dated shortly before he died."

The look on Keenan's face didn't bother her one bit; she dealt with this type of male many times.

Sheriff Long pulled himself together and changed from a puzzled man into the take-charge kind of guy he wished he was. He didn't need this. He stood to signal the meeting was done.

"When would it be convenient for me to pick up the files, assuming you don't have them with you?"

"Oh, we don't have them with us, but we could drop them off sometime tomorrow," Athena quickly answered. She knew Beth was not keen on having him in Martin's office.

"OK, that's fine, give me a call, I'll be sure to be here," Sheriff Long said. "The sooner the better. I'm sure you ladies have some shopping or whatever to do. Nice of you to stop by."

Beth knew this was her exit cue.

As they walked out she couldn't help but take a glance at the desk where her husband had parked his lanky frame for all those years. The desk looked the same but it now belonged to someone else. She tried to smile but she choked. It was just too painful. The women didn't talk until they reached the car. Beth was the first to speak.

"Whew, that wasn't as easy as I thought it would be," she said.

"I'm not too sure about this sheriff, I don't think I like him. He isn't very professional," Athena said. "The deputy is cute but he's stuck on himself. I think his main job is keeping the sheriff out of hot water."

As they pulled out of the parking lot Beth's thoughts were focused on Martin's files and the best way to get rid of them. Athena was thinking of a way to utilize them for a new book, which meant hanging on to them for a while.

On the drive to pick up Missy, both women were silent. Suddenly, both began to speak at once. Through a few tears and hand squeezes, they apologized to one another, the first time they had discussed the flare-up of the other day.

"We're sisters, honey, and blood comes first," Athena said. "I'm here to help, so I'll try to mind my big-city ways around you."

"Oh Athena, maybe you're right," Beth said. "Those guys look as if they couldn't solve a crossword puzzle. Go ahead and try to write that book. Who knows? You may find out something that's been staring them in the face."

They picked up Missy on the way home. It was about 5:30 when they eased the car into the driveway. Missy ran straight up to her room. "She's probably already on her computer checking out Facebook," Beth laughed as the women headed up to Martin's office.

Beth pushed open the door and gasped. The place was a wreck. Someone had been there, looking for something. The computer was gone, files were all over the floor and the closet that held the gun safe was wide open. But the safe wasn't touched. Looking at each other, they turned and rushed up to Missy's room.

"Thank God you're safe," Beth said, grabbing her daughter and pulling her back down the stairs.

"Mom, what's going on? I was talking to—"

"—Never you mind," Beth snapped.

Her cell phone was out of her purse before she got to the car. She punched in the preprogrammed number for the sheriff's office. Sheriff Long answered. Beth quickly explained what they discovered.

"Stay in your car, don't go back into the house; I'll be right there."

The sheriff and deputy made it to Beth's in less than 10 minutes. Beth, Missy, and Athena remained in the car away from the crime scene.

After the initial examination of the room the sheriff and the deputy were both perplexed. It seemed to be a very clean job, aside from the files thrown around on the floor. No typical trail of prints and broken locks that were usually left by kids or smash and grab robbers. Nothing of value except the computer was missing. Dusting for prints turned up very little. Keenan had an uneasy feeling about this; it didn't seem as innocent as a simple break-in.

"I'm so sorry this happened, Beth. I believe it was just some wild-ass kids, excuse my French, we'll find them," Sheriff Long said. Was he trying to convince himself or her? He gave her a complete incident report and a stern warning about setting her alarm every time she left the house.

"He'll find them?" Athena scoffed as the sheriff and Keenan drove off. "He couldn't find his behind with both hands."

CHAPTER 7: Tuesday, November 9

Athena found it hard to sleep. At 4:30 in the morning, she lay in bed, a table lamp lighting the legal pad on her chest. She started to write. At first, slowly, and then faster, she listed all the things that had gone on in town since she arrived. Somehow she knew they were not random occurrences. However, connecting them would take an effort.

She thanked her lucky stars they still had the flash drive from Martin's office. Putting the flash drive in the Altoids box had been a stroke of luck. The thief apparently had knocked it to the floor where it landed under the recliner; still closed and safe.

The computer would be easy to replace and the insurance agent had assured Beth that a settlement would be made as soon as possible. The file folders that had been taken were just an inconvenience.

"Beth must be going out of her mind," she said out loud. Thinking ahead to tomorrow, she began to list questions only Beth could answer. With her sister's help, things might look clearer in the morning; they were pretty cloudy right now.

She knew Beth was trying to keep her sanity while everything around her seemed to be spinning out of control. I wish there was another way, maybe Sheriff Long could shed some light on the subject for me, she thought, and wondered if he would. After a while she ran out of questions and ideas, so she turned out the light. In the early morning hours she drifted off to a sleep of nightmares. Someone was lurking, and she couldn't see his face. He stayed in the shadows and never left.

Aroused by a flood of sunlight, she opened her eyes. She felt tired, as if she hadn't slept, and the vision of the intruder from her nightmare was fresh in her mind. She picked up the pen and tablet that had dropped beside the bed. This yellow pad of paper brought back more anxiety; she had written quite a lot before sleep captured her.

With a cup of coffee and Beth's input she could rejuvenate her mind. Or at least she could put the events in chronological order; she worked better with less chaos. The kids had left for school and Beth was staring out the kitchen window when Athena walked in.

As unobtrusively as possible she said, "Good morning, Beth."

"Good morning, sis," Beth answered without turning around.

There was another legal pad on the table, so Athena laid hers near it, poured herself some coffee and sat down. "Last night my mind was dashing from one thing to another so fast I would have bet I wouldn't sleep a wink," she said. "I did and I had nightmares about the break-in all night. Did you get any rest?"

"You know, Martin planted this hibiscus under the kitchen window the first year we were here," Beth said in a voice so soft that Athena could hardly hear her. "They were his favorites and mine too. Yellow reminds me of sunshine."

Athena instinctively knew her sister hadn't had a good night and now wished she had sat with her longer last night. She remembered how, when they were kids and things got bad, Beth would tune out, change the subject, and remove herself from the pain.

Athena walked to the sink and put her arm around her sister. She could feel the tension in her body.

"They are beautiful," Athena said as she looked at the flowers. "Everyone has red ones in their yards, but these are the largest ones I've ever seen, and the color, well, sunshine was never this vivid."

She wouldn't bring up the break-in until Beth was ready. "The coffee is good and it's just what I need," Athena continued to try to get Beth talking. "Do you want a refill?"

Beth held her cup out in answer to the question. She smiled. Gradually she was coming back.

The sisters took their cups to the table. Side by side lay the two yellow pads. Beth's had nothing written on it.

"Athena, I just want this to go away, I can't keep doing this," Beth said. "But I know I need to do something."

Athena was surprised by this decision. She needed Beth's help, at least right now, so the change of heart gratified her.

"Beth, I'm sorry. I don't mean to cause you any more stress," Athena said. "You know it isn't going away until we can find a few answers; help me if you can and I'll do what I can to help you. Take a look at this." With that, Athena showed her the questions she needed help with.

1- James Jenkins arrives in CC not knowing about his brother, a stranger in town. CC didn't know about him, why?

2- He gets the news about his family. I wonder why no one knew about him, where had he been, where does he live. Prison?

3- He appears on TV. Asks for help, seems to be in shock about his family, and seems very determined to find out anything he can.

4- We find files about Frank Jenkins. Don't know if they are complete. There are police reports, autopsies, interviews, and pictures. Was Martin working on these or just cleaning up files?

5- Sheriff opens up old case. We visit sheriff and tell him about finding files on Martin's computer. He's not much help.

6- Martin's office is broken into. Computer is stolen, what happened to the missing gun?

7- Sheriff wants all Martin's files.

"Don't these things make you wonder what's going on?" Athena said. "Let's find some answers to these questions. We can do that, I'm sure."

"I'm as ready as I'll ever be, let's get on with it," Beth said.

The phone rang.

"Hello," Beth answered.

"Beth?" said Sheriff Long. "Sorry to call so early, but I wanted to reach you before you went out today. Would it be possible to come over to see you this morning? I really need to talk to you, but I'd rather not have you come to the office."

"I'm sitting here with my sister and as a matter of fact, we were just thinking about you, too," Beth said. "Come over now. I'll make a fresh pot of coffee."

"I'm waiting for James Jenkins, but as soon as he's come and gone I'll be on my way."

* * *

As Beth and Athena pored over their notes, James was arriving right on time for his meeting with the sheriff. Keenan met him and ushered him to the conference room.

"Hello, James," Sheriff Long said. "You look like you haven't been sleeping. I just want you to know, we are on your family's case. I'm making Keenan number one man, as far as this investigation goes."

"We'll keep you up to date as much as we can," Keenan said. "Have a seat. Can I get you some coffee or water or a cold soda?"

"Thanks, I'll have a Coke," James replied. "Has something new come up?" he said, looking at Sheriff Long. He was glad Deputy McDuff was going to be number one man, whatever that meant.

"No, not yet," Sheriff Long answered, as Keenan stepped out to get a soda.

The two men sat in silence, waiting for Keenan to return.

"Here you go," Keenan said as he returned. James opened the beverage and eyed both men, his heart pounding. What did they want?

"Yesterday was pretty hectic around here and if we came across as uncaring, I apologize." Keenan was going to treat him with kid gloves.

"We are officially re-opening this case," Sheriff Long said, needing to put his own two cents in. "James, this conversation is going to be recorded, as a matter of procedure. Just want you to know."

James nodded. That was certainly OK with him. Maybe they were starting to treat this like a real case. "I wasn't even here then, I don't know what I can add." He didn't have any answers, only questions.

Sheriff Long hit the record button on the out-of-date recorder. He guessed that would be his job now.

"Tell me about your brother, did he have any vices, any enemies, or any other relatives we missed? How we missed you as a relative I don't know. Nothing is too remote, and it could lead us in a different direction." Keenan was using his friendliest tone. And James could sure use a friend.

James answered as honestly as he could.

"Frankie was a friendly guy. I hadn't seen him in five years; a lot can happen in five years. Before that, he was just a young man trying to get along in this world."

Something was bugging Keenan. "Why didn't anyone here in Citrus City know Frankie had a brother?"

"Frankie and I had a falling out when I was arrested. I'm sure you've already checked my record. Frankie said he didn't ever want to see me again." James took a long drink of his soda. "I let him down, I'm sorry. I loved my brother, he was all I had. I let him and his family down. Maybe if I had been around five years ago—"

Sheriff Long was touched by this show of emotion.

"Take your time," Keenan said. "And don't blame yourself; we'll do all we can to find the bad guy."

"I'll help any way I can! I can't rest until I have some answers! Are my brother and his family buried around here? I'd like to see the graves."

"Mr. Parnell provided for them," Sheriff Long said. "They are buried at the First Baptist Church. He paid for the service and the plot. He even has flowers delivered each year on the anniversary."

"Why didn't he hire someone to take over Frankie's job?" James asked. "It seems the house is falling down and there's nothing out there, the road is almost grown over. My guess is it's just like Frankie left it,"

"It is," the sheriff said. "I guess Parnell lost interest in it after all this; he didn't even try to sell it. Don't exactly know why. It has been in the Parnell family for many years. I'll ask him on our next interview."

"James, I will promise you this; we will work on this until there's nothing left to discover," Keenan said as he stood up. "Thanks for coming in."

Sheriff Long hit the stop button on the recorder and stood also.

James didn't want to go, but he couldn't stay here.

"I'm not leaving town so you will see a lot of me, and thanks," James said. "By the way, I'm looking for a job, do you know of anything? I can't afford to stay at the Days Inn much longer."

"You might try Shorty's. If he can't help you he might know who can," Sheriff Long said. "He knows everything going on in town."

As James left, Sheriff Long turned to Keenan and said, "I need to step out of the office for a while. Hold down the fort; I won't be gone long."

Twenty minutes later, he parked in Beth's driveway. Sheriff Long left his hat on the front seat as he exited the county issued vehicle. The seasonal breeze mussed his comb-over hair style just a little. He reached up and smoothed it down, looked around to be sure no one had followed him, and walked determinedly to the front door.

Beth opened the door before Sheriff Long had a chance to knock.

"Good morning, Sheriff, come on in."

"Howdy ma'am!"

He followed her through the living room to the kitchen.

"And yes, I'll have that cup of Joe," he said before she asked.

"Morning, Athena," he said glancing her way.

"Good morning, Sheriff."

Pouring coffee for the sheriff, Beth asked, "Cream and sugar?"

"Thanks, I'll take it black," he said.

Beth sat his cup on the table across from her sister and Sheriff Long took his seat.

"You make the best coffee in town, smells great," he said. "Are both you ladies doing OK? Sometimes after a break-in, people are afraid to stay in the house."

"We're all right," Beth answered. Beth and Athena had discussed the sheriff's request to come over and were a little confused by it. "Are there any new developments?" Beth asked. "Did you catch whoever did this?"

"Well, no, but I'm really worried about you. I'm going to have Tom drive by your house several times when he is on nights. I didn't want you worrying when you see the squad car in the area."

"Thanks, Sheriff, I appreciate that," Beth said. "I know Martin would appreciate your concern, but would you mind telling me why you didn't want me coming by the office this morning?"

"Um, I thought I would save you the trip," he said.

Athena looked skeptical.

He continued. "One other thing; all the files I saw after your break-in were duplicates, so if you could shred them, I'd be grateful. No sense taking them to the office, they'd just take up what extra space we have and it looks like we'll be needing that space."

"I can do that," she replied. That was the best idea he had come up with yet, she thought. Athena was still silent, still observing the sheriff. Something else was definitely on his mind. He beat around the bush until he couldn't put it off any longer.

"And another thing, on this murder investigation, you ladies need to let us do our jobs. Don't you worry your pretty little heads about it."

There it was; his real reason for the trip to their house.

Sheriff Long finished his drink, put his cup in the sink and headed for the door. "Well, I'd better be going. You know you can call me, and if we have anything new to report about the break-in, believe me, we'll call you. Now have a nice day."

With Sheriff Long gone, Beth and Athena just sat there and they looked at each other. A moment later they broke into laughter. When they quieted, they felt better.

"Pretty little heads? Is he telling us to butt out?" Athena said. "What is he trying to say? Does he think we are getting in his way?"

"I hate to say this," Beth said, "but I think they bungled the first investigation. Martin probably knew it too. But it is just now coming out. They must be worried, especially with that Jenkins boy going on TV and all. I'm beginning to wonder why Martin was working on this alone, not sharing anything with Long. Not that Long is any help."

"I have an idea," Athena said.

"You and your ideas will get us in trouble," Beth replied.

"We should find this James Jenkins," Athena said. James could be a good lead character and a wealth of information for her book. He had been in prison, and he was dealing with a violent crime. "Maybe we could talk to him. I don't think it would hurt, but let's be discreet. We probably shouldn't let the sheriff know that we are doing anything connected to the case.

Beth picked up the phone and handed it to her sister. "If anybody could talk to James Jenkins, it's you."

CHAPTER 8: Wednesday, November 10

Cleveland Parnell stood near the windows of his seventh-story office in Chicago's Loop. His office was large by any standard. His antique desk was huge, too big for conventionally-sized offices. The chair had been purchased from an auction house in London years ago by his father. The Persian rug was a crowning touch. Parnell worked better in a well-appointed space.

Looking down, everyone on the streets below him was small and insignificant. The morning rush hour was well under way and throngs of early workers, all with their heads down, scurried in the cold morning air. Although it was cold, the sun was trying to peek over the buildings to the east of him. Parnell was an early riser and worked best in the morning. Some people have problems getting up early; not him, so he was always in the office long before his secretary and staff.

The downtown streets and windows were already decorated for the holidays. He had been in a festive mood until the phone call. Sheriff Long from Florida wanted to set up an appointment to re-interview him on a very old case.

The sheriff's call caught him off guard. But he promised he would be ready for the phone interview. Sheriff Long wanted him to fly down for a face-to-face meeting about the Jenkins case. It was all he could do not to laugh out loud. Big things were shaping up in Chicago, what with the mayoral election and a few business moves that were about to pop. The last thing he needed was a trip to Mayberry. So there he was, waiting for the sheriff's call.

The Jenkins case was the last thing on his mind this morning. The five-year old murders had ended up in the cold case files. That was where he expected it to stay. Now Long says, "something new has come up. We are reopening the case and we need to re-interview you. It's just a formality." Formality my ass, he thought. The last thing he needed was that can of worms being reopened. After all this time, what could persuade Long to reopen this case?

Parnell glanced away from the ever-increasing herd of people on the sidewalk below. His eyes darkened and his mind jumped back five years.

When Frank Jenkins was killed, he had just picked up his Christmas bonus and then hurried home to his death. He liked Frank; he was perfect for the job. Never asked questions, wasn't capable of much. But then, not much was expected of him. His death should not have happened.

Soon enough, at 9 a.m. the buzzer sounded.

"Call for you on line 12, Mr. Parnell," chirped Suzy.

"Put it through," snapped Parnell.

"Morning, gentlemen," he said a moment later.

"Morning, Mr. Parnell," Sheriff Long said. That man even *sounds* nervous. Well, thought Parnell, I helped put him where he is, he'd better be nervous.

"Mr. Parnell, I have my deputy, Keenan McDuff on speaker phone here, if that's all right with you, sir."

Parnell was about to say no, it's not all right, just to see what would happen. But he needed to get this over with, so he just grunted.

"Do you mind if we record this?" the sheriff asked. "It will help us with our notes and we probably won't need to bother you again."

Parnell never allowed any conversation he was a part of to be recorded, unless he was the one recording it. But, under the circumstances, he agreed. These small town boys had a lot to learn.

After stating the date and identifying each one present by name, the sheriff was ready to begin.

"As you may or may not know, there has been a new development in the Jenkins case," the sheriff said. "Frank's brother, James, who was in prison for about five years, just got out and came here looking for his brother. Somehow we never knew Frank Jenkins had a brother, so James Jenkins wasn't notified at the death. Did you know Frank had a brother, Mr. Parnell?"

Parnell was genuinely surprised with this news. How had he missed this? "No, I didn't. Frank was my employee but I didn't know much about his personal life. I did know about the wife and kids. I like to keep things at a distance, especially where my employees are concerned," Parnell said, trying to sound very open with the sheriff because this was the truth. His Chicago employees were different ducks; he made it a point to know everything about them.

"Have you had any dealing with anyone who might have a grudge against you; had there been any problems on the ranch?" Long asked.

Parnell winced. I deal with all kinds of people and problems on a daily basis, and I mean deal! What is Long thinking, is he that naive?

"No, no problems on the ranch. I do business with a lot of people, none of whom have anything against me; you're barking up the wrong tree. This is all about Frank, I'm sure you will find that out, one way or another. My business up north is an entirely different organization, I don't mix the two."

Keenan butted in. "Why didn't you hire someone to oversee the place, someone to take Frank's place, Mr. Parnell? The ranch is run down and hasn't been operational since."

Who is this wiseass kid? Parnell thought.

"The truth is, this killing put me in total shock and I just lost interest. I sold the cattle and horses and never hired anyone after that. I'm thinking of renting out the land; it's just a thought, nothing confirmed."

This phone conference lasted another hour; nothing new was detected. Parnell noticed the sheriff deferred to the McDuff fellow, who seemed to be a little sharper than the usual Citrus City lawman.

"Thank you so much for talking to us, Mr. Parnell," Sheriff Long said. "And we will keep you up to date on anything that turns up. Sorry to take up so much of your time."

Parnell signed off and then looked at his cell phone. He needed to check his messages. Long was a bother and an annoying inconvenience. And this new deputy, he could be trouble. He was smarter and more educated; Parnell could tell that immediately. His only surprise was the appearance of Frank's brother. Parnell didn't like surprises; they gave you a disadvantage.

No new messages. He called Dominick Trivino, his silent partner for the last ten years. The mutual relationship worked well. Dom had connections in this town that went back years and Parnell had the money. Not too many things happened without Dom's approval, and few things happened without Parnell's money—politics as usual in the Windy City.

"Dom, what's the status on the election, and the merger?"

"I need to see you in person," Dom replied. "You know how I hate these phones. What about lunch? You're buying."

Parnell hung up the phone, hoping this face-to-face didn't mean a problem. He'd be there, Dino's at noon. This was the routine, their second office. How he wished for the good old days. Where were the Daleys, either one of them, when you needed them? Oh well, the new mayoral candidate still had time to lose the election. Elections were set for the last Tuesday in February. It's only November, we just have our work cut out for us, or, rather, Dom does.

Parnell told his secretary to hold all calls. He needed uninterrupted concentration for a few hours before meeting Trivino. The Citrus City thing had Cleveland Parnell agitated. Who was this brother of Jenkins? Just another loser? he speculated after the phone conference. I better do some research on the new deputy.

At his computer, he typed in "Jenkins, James." Going to the right data base he saw James's background, arrest record, release date, and little else. His secretary could do this much faster than he could. However, he didn't trust her to know he kept a personal file on everyone he worked with.

He printed the information, jotted down a few details on an index card, and then placed the larger file in a locked drawer where he kept personal information.

Parnell was surprised at the education and experience of McDuff, as he was young and he was from the South. He was a college graduate and had worked in Tampa for a few years. He had transferred to Citrus City six months ago after the death of Deputy Martin Filmore, who had died in an auto accident. Looking at this information made Parnell realize he wasn't very current on events in his home town.

He placed the index card with information on James Jenkins and Keenan McDuff in his pocket, then turned back to the business of the city.

Before he realized it, 11:45 loomed; time to meet Dom. He was soon on his way. The air was downright cold. He thought once more about Citrus City, where it would probably be almost balmy this late in the season. The lunch crowd was just starting to form at Dino's, but that wasn't a problem for Cleveland Parnell. He walked past the maitre d' directly to the private dining room in the rear.

"Good afternoon, Mr. Parnell," the head waiter said with a respectful nod of the head. "Mr. Trivino is waiting for you."

"Thank you, Tony," he replied

"What'll it be?" Dom asked, as Parnell entered. "The good vino or the cheap stuff?"

"You tell me," Parnell answered. "What's it look like, did you meet with the mayor or not? Can we celebrate or are we drinking to forget?"

"Let's go with the good stuff!" Dom said. He snapped his fingers and a young Italian man appeared almost instantly. "Bring us the wine Enzo picked out!" Dom told the waiter. Enzo had been around long before Dom acquired the restaurant and his choices were always correct. Within a few minutes the wine was served and the waiter disappeared. As usual, Dom liked to prolong the introduction of business. The first glass of wine was a ceremony in his eyes. So Parnell smiled, leaned back, and enjoyed the wine.

"Good choice," he said. When their glasses were empty the waiter appeared automatically, with more wine.

After he left, Dom leaned in close. "Our friend, the mayor, has assured me that we can count on the contract. It is being approved even as we speak. All that's needed is your signature to clinch it. As for the election, well, let's say, I'm still working on it. Either way, we will be victorious, as they say in the movies! Now, my friend, you look as if a weight occupies your mind, something beyond our Windy City affairs."

Parnell smiled. "I have a small job for you. Here are the names of two people I need to know more about. Number one is the new deputy in Citrus City and number two is the long lost brother of my former ranch hand." He brought Dom up to date on Frankie's murder and the day's phone conference. As Cleveland had already accessed his computer for public information, he now needed personal data. The deep search. He knew he would have the necessary information by tomorrow.

Dom took the three-by five-card Cleveland offered him, looked at it and put it in his pocket. This was one of the things Parnell liked about his partner; he didn't ask questions.

"Let's order!"

Both men picked up their personal menus at the same time, meeting adjourned. They made their lunch decisions immediately. Too bad business wasn't as cut and dried.

* * *

Meanwhile, back in Citrus City, Sheriff Long and McDuff reviewed the conversation with Parnell.

"Well, it looks like that was a dead end," Sheriff Long said. He was still sweating. Speaking to a heavyweight like Parnell reminded him of his place in the pecking order.

"I don't know about that," McDuff answered.

"What do you mean?" Sheriff Long asked.

"Well, you say this Cleveland Parnell is a big-time businessman, right?"

"That's right," Sheriff Long said. "He owns a lot of property around here and from what I understand he's a real go-getter up there in Chicago."

"If he's such a go-getter, why would he pack up his tent and quit right after the murders?" Keenan asked. "Wouldn't a guy like that want to get to the bottom of things? Wouldn't he want some answers?"

'What are you trying to say?" Sheriff Long asked.

"Just that we shouldn't just write him off," Keenan said. "What if it was in his interest to keep things hush-hush? What if there was a reason for him being so quick to let sleeping dogs lie?"

"Now wait just a minute," Sheriff Long said, rising from his desk. "I've known the Parnell family for years, and I won't sit here and let some young Wyatt Earp wannabe talk bad about them based on a hunch."

It didn't take much for the sheriff to get upset; McDuff's insinuations spoke both to his personal sense of propriety and his abilities as a sheriff. Who was he to assume the department had rolled over for Parnell?

McDuff held up his hands. "Whoa, chief, I didn't mean to get you riled up. But let me ask you this. You say you've known Parnell for years; how long had you known Frank Jenkins?"

"Ever since he moved here," Sheriff Long sputtered. "But what does that have to do with—"

"Just this," McDuff snapped. "Frank Jenkins deserves justice; he deserves the same consideration that this Parnell guy expects." McDuff looked up at Sheriff Long, his blue eyes flashing. "Frank's lying in a grave next to his wife and kids with his murder unsolved, and all this Parnell guy can think about is the inconvenience. That's not right."

Sheriff Long paused, then sat down. He thought about Frank Jenkins, his little family, and the bloody crime scene. At heart he was a decent man and nothing McDuff had said about Parnell hit him as hard as the deputy's last words, "that's not right."

"No, son," Sheriff Long sighed. "It ain't right." He thought about it a moment. "So what do we do now?"

CHAPTER 9: Friday, November 12

On Tuesday, when Athena had reached James, he had agreed to see them Friday afternoon. That worked for them, as it gave them time to think about what they wanted to accomplish. But when the day arrived, Beth had second thoughts.

"Why do I let you talk me into things?" Beth asked when Athena picked up the car keys.

"Because deep down you need to know," Athena replied.

"We don't know this guy; I don't think we can help him," Beth said. "You're just doing this because of that stupid book you're going to write. What are we going to do? Just ask him questions? I've changed my mind. You go by yourself."

"Come on, we said we'd be there," Athena said. "We can't just not show."

Reluctantly, Beth followed Athena to the car. If nothing else, she thought, at least I'm getting out of the house, It was a short drive to Days Inn; just a few miles north of town. They had gone over the information found on Martin's computer and devised a plan to share with James, depending on his response.

In the parking lot, neither women wanted to be the first one out of the car.

"What are we doing?" Beth said.

"Going to see James Jenkins in his hotel room," Athena replied. She started to laugh. "This is crazy! I haven't been to a man's hotel room in a long time. I'll bet this is a first for you."

"What if he is a serial killer, what if he is a rapist?" Beth asked. "What was he in prison for?"

"Safety in numbers, remember that karate class you took? Maybe you'll get a chance to use it. Come on."

"I also know how to use a gun," Beth said with a small smile. "OK, tell me again, why do you think this James guy can help?"

"We are here (A) because we can't depend on Frick and Frack to handle this, and we need answers," Athena said, as if checking off a list. "(B), I'd like to take some notes for my book, and (C), we don't have anyone else. Besides, Martin would be proud of you.

He was looking for answers in this case. Wouldn't he try to talk to James Jenkins?"

"Martin would think we were nuts!" Beth answered.

They tapped on the door. James opened it expectantly. He had shaved and combed his very short hair. His mother always said," First impressions are lasting ones." He was glad he had made the effort. What he saw surprised him. There stood two attractive women coming to his aid.

As they entered, they noticed the room was small with a double bed that took up most of the space. A table with two chairs sat in front of the window. The drapes were wide open and the afternoon sun light was streaming in. It was clean and neat.

The look on James Jenkins's face was the first thing Athena noticed. He was polite and didn't seem to be intimidated by having two women, whom he didn't know, in his room. Athena also noticed that he was much better looking in person than on TV. He was in clean jeans and a T-shirt, and she immediately recognized the biceps of a man who worked out.

"First of all, I'm sincerely sorry for your loss. This has to be terrible for you," Athena said, looking into a face that was handsome and expectant.

"Let me start by getting this off my chest," James said. "I hope you are here to help. Please say yes. I think the sheriff's office screwed up, plain and simple.

I don't know if they can help or not. I really don't know if they want to help."

Beth and Athena were a little surprised that the three of them were already on the same wavelength.

"You may be right. My husband, Martin, was a deputy who worked on the case." Beth paused long enough for this to soak in.

"I'm sorry, I didn't mean any disrespect for him, as a matter of fact I haven't met him yet," James said. "I've only met Sheriff Long and his deputies, McDuff and Wiley."

"Martin died six month ago in a car accident," Beth said.

"Oh my God, sorry, I'm so sorry. I don't know what to say." They could see James was indeed sympathetic. Get a grip, he thought, this won't help anyone! He sat on the edge of the bed and gestured to them to take the two chairs. Looking from one woman to the other, he tried to compose himself. So far, in this town, he had met only two people he considered nice. One sold him a car, the other was Deputy McDuff. Maybe the women were two more people he could trust.

As he talked, Athena checked him out. His well-defined muscles flexed every time he moved. Athena looked at those muscles, and thought about everything she had heard about prison. Suddenly a ripple of fear coursed through her—she was in a tiny room with a man who had survived Florida State Prison. But then she thought of Truman Capote, her literary hero, and how he grew close enough to two murderers to write *In Cold Blood*. If he could do it, she thought, conjuring up an image of the effeminate writer, then I can.

"Let's try to see if we can help, James," Athena said. "Right now we're all grasping at straws."

Beth jumped right in. "Three days ago, right after you got in town, my house was broken into."

My God, he thought, do they think I did it?

"We were cleaning my husband's office and found a lot of files about Frank," Beth continued. "After I told the sheriff about the files, someone broke in and stole the computer, among other things. It seems strange that Martin's office was the only room touched. Sheriff Long tried to convince me it was just some kids, but I'm not buying it."

James looked at both women. He felt like a jerk for thinking they suspected him. He could see that their compassion was real. Plus he hadn't seen two more attractive women in a long, long time. The younger one was petite, with nice, long brown hair. But it was the older woman who stopped James in his tracks. She had a hairstyle that framed her face, with golden streaks throughout. Her skin seemed to glow and her eyes sparkled. She had a womanly shape that her baggy blouse and loose jeans didn't hide. Get a grip, he thought, that's not what they're here for.

"I don't want to think anyone would have reason to kill my brother and his family, but they did," he said, trying to get his mind off the wrong thing.

"Do you know the owner of the property, a Mr. Parnell? I'd really like to talk to him," James said.

"I don't know Parnell, but I know of him," Beth answered. "He's very rich. Parnell is from Chicago and spends most of his time there. He owns a big house west of town, just a few miles from the ranch. The ranch and the house, it's been in his family for years. The sheriff likes him, as a matter of fact, Martin used to say that when Parnell was in town, which wasn't very often, Sheriff Long stayed in the office so he could be on call if needed. It seemed Parnell never needed him."

The more they talked, the more Athena was drawn to James. She really wanted to help him.

"I wonder if I could find out anything about him for you," she said. "I'm from Chicago, I'll see if people I know have ever heard of him. I have a friend who is a reporter for the *Chicago Tribune*. She might be able to find out something about him. It's worth a try."

"You're from Chicago? What are you doing here?" James asked. He liked looking at Athena, she was good to look at and smart. "I'll bet it's cold up there already." What a stupid thing to say, he thought, get back to the issues at hand.

"I don't have any faith in the sheriff," James said. "But Keenan seems pretty sharp. He seems concerned. I think if I could see Keenan without Long it might go better. I'm gonna try."

"How are you going to do that?" Beth asked, wondering if Keenan would be open to it.

"I'll just call him, he said call if I need anything, well, I need something now," James said. "I have a cell phone. Here's my number."

Athena took this opportunity to give James her phone number, too. He was shaping up to be a better than expected source for her book.

"What's your next step?" she asked.

"Well, I found out from Sheriff Long that the family is buried in the cemetery at the Baptist Church," James said, his blue eyes fixed directly on her. "I'm taking a trip out there Sunday afternoon."

She stared back. Why is he looking at me like that? Athena thought. "We'll continue going over our notes," she said nervously. "I'll call my friend in Chicago to see what I can find out about Cleveland Parnell."

"Thank you both so much, I feel better today than I've felt since I arrived here," James said. Holding his phone up and looking at it as if it were something special he said, "Call me!" Then his demeanor changed. "Let's keep this between us for now."

That's just what Beth and Athena were thinking.

* * *

"James is sincere about not giving up on finding his brother's killer," Athena said as the women left the Days Inn.

"Can you blame him?" Beth said. "Sorry I didn't trust your instincts about talking to James."

"That's OK, I was a little worried myself," Athena conceded. "I'm glad we didn't have to rely on what you learned in karate class, or gun class for that matter. Do they call it gun class or what?" she added.

"It's called target practice or shooting range. But what do you city girls know about guns?" Beth joked.

"You haven't been to Chicago lately," Athena laughed. "I could use some target practice myself. When we get home, I'll call my friend at the *Tribune* and see if she has ever heard of Cleveland Parnell. I've never heard of him, myself, but I don't keep up with the in crowd. I'm more in tune with the literary types. Chances are he doesn't make the front page often."

The visit had done both women good. The tension caused by reopening the old wounds of Martin's death had been eased by their shared concern that justice had yet to be served.

"Getting back to James," Beth said. "Do you think Martin would approve of all this investigating?"

"I wouldn't call it investigating, more like doing research," Athena said. "And I do think Martin would want this unfinished business brought to some kind of closure."

"OK," Beth said.

As soon as they were home, they went to Martin's office.

"You can work from here, maybe Martin would like that," Beth said.

Since the break-in they had removed the file cabinets. Goodwill was only too happy to pick them up. And Beth had added a round glass top table in front of the large east windows. Her HGTV vision was becoming a reality. She had placed a floral arrangement on the table, giving it a homier feel. With the new area rug she liked the look and feel of the room. The laptop computer was new and the closet still housed the guns, but Beth hoped to find a buyer for them before too long.

She felt a pang of remorse; redecorating the room was like exorcising Martin's spirit. But she knew her husband; he would have wanted her to move on. Besides, Martin would always live in her heart. No amount of redecorating would ever change that.

Athena looked up the number of her friend, Jessica Sinclair. Jessica was a columnist who covered politics as well as many other things in Chicago.

"Hello, Athena," Jessica said.

"Hi, Jess, long time no see," Athena said.

"No, I don't have time for lunch, but if you're buying I could tear myself away." They both laughed, remembering their fun times together.

"Jess, I'm in Florida, paradise at my fingertips, why would I want to have lunch where the weather is 40 degrees? It's going to be 80 here today," she said, fudging on the temperature just a little.

"Oh, girl, that's all I need to hear," Jess moaned. "What's up?"

She and Athena had been friends for years, even before Athena was married. They had met back when Athena was a budding writer of children's books, trying to get published.

"You know a lot of people in the city, right?" Athena started. "Well I'm looking for some info, anything you can find, on a well-heeled Chicago guy with a home in Florida. Think you could help?"

"I'll try; you want to know if he is married, what he does for a living, is he available, right?"

"No, nothing like that," Athena laughed. "Well maybe."

"Ok, what's his name?" Jessica said.

"Cleveland Parnell."

"Wow, I thought you had a hard question!" Jessica said. "This one is easy. Parnell is pretty well-known here; although he does like to fly under the radar. He's involved in politics; he's a money man behind the scenes. He's a personal friend of the mayor, too. Let me do a little research and get back to you! Maybe I'll bring the report to you. I'm not ready for winter yet."

"Thanks a lot, I owe you big time. I'll be back in the city before long. Stay warm and I'll wait to hear from you."

After hanging up, Athena turned to Beth and said, "After we hear from Jess, we'll know more. Don't know if it will help or not. In the meantime, I'll work on this information, try to organize it better."

Athena stared out the window into the serene woods. "I can't help but see James Jenkins's face," she said. "He seems like an OK guy. You can see how devastated he is. He doesn't have a friend in the world and his family is gone. I really feel sorry for him."

"Are you sure it's just his predicament?" Beth asked. "I noticed a little chemistry going on there, Miss Cougar."

"Miss Cougar? What are you talking about, Beth?"

"You know, that's what the kids call women who chase after younger men."

"Are you kidding?" Athena blushed. "I'm old enough to be his—well, old enough to be his big sister. Besides, he's great material for the book."

They had nothing in common, she thought. He was younger than her, he was an ex-con, and although he seemed nice, Athena doubted she could chat about books or foreign policy with him.

"Little sister knows big sister a little too well," Beth said.

"You wish," Athena replied. They both laughed. Beth thought about why she had called Athena to come down in the first place. She was more organized, better at getting things done, and better at making decisions. Beth expected her older sister to hold her hand and help her rebuild her life without Martin. Athena's take-charge manner, while at first offensive, had lifted Beth out of self-pity. Now, watching her older sister blush like a teenager, Beth remembered the good times they shared and loved her sister all the more.

Instinctively she hugged Athena. Softly she said, "All joking aside, what's our next step?"

Athena smiled. "Well, I think I have a date at a graveyard come Sunday."

"You are kidding, right?" Beth asked. But she knew Athena meant what she said.

CHAPTER 10: Sunday, November 14

Athena checked herself again in the rear-view mirror. After changing her clothes twice before she left, she still wasn't sure she should have worn her Vera Wang slacks. But they did look great on her. Her blouse was pastel blue; she had only worn it one other time in Chicago. It was comfortable, it was a good color for her, and it showed off her curves. She smiled and thought, I haven't spent this much time worrying about how I look in a long time.

Athena was excited about today. She'd be able to see James in his element, grieving for his family. Part of her felt as if she was exploiting him, like one of those buzzards you see on the side of the road picking at dead armadillos. But her writer's side stifled those concerns. She kidded herself into thinking she was just going to help a man who truly needed help. And Beth needed closure on this issue, since it was definitely something Martin wanted. As a writer, Athena was good at putting things in order. The more facts she had the better the ending would be. There, she had completely justified the visit to see James.

The church was easy to find, since she had accessed the map on her tablet. Straight down 2nd Street, you couldn't miss it. She pulled into the lot and parked under a sprawling oak. The church was not very big and neither was the cemetery. Church services were over and only one car remained in the lot.

Looking around, she saw a lone figure sitting under a large pine tree. The silhouette looked familiar. It was a man and he was bent over holding his head; praying, crying, maybe both. Silently, she walked up to him. Should I speak or walk by? It only took a minute to decide. This is why I'm here.

"Hello, James," she said softly.

James jerked his head up. Backlit by the sun, Athena's face was indistinct, but the glare gave her a glow, almost as if a halo encircled her head. Her perfume filled his nostrils. For James, who had gone too long without the company of women, it was as if an angel had appeared. He stared, open-mouthed.

"James?" she said again.

"I'm sorry," he said, snapping out of his rapture. "I—I—"

"I didn't mean to disturb you," Athena said softly. I've never had a man look at me that way, she thought.

"No, no, it's all right. I was just—I thought I saw—I was just sitting here thinking. Have a seat."

"If I'm infringing on your private time, just say so, I'll come back later," Athena offered.

"Stay, please stay," James said. Was this real? He smiled as she sat down beside him. "With the sun behind your back, I thought you—aw, don't mind me, I'm just hallucinating, I guess. This is the quietest place in town; when I'm here, I can't hear the gossip or feel the stares of people wondering if I'm here to cause trouble."

Athena hadn't seen a man cry in many years. It moved her and, for some reason, it excited her too.

"The headstones are very nice, but I'm still having trouble believing Frankie is gone. Have you ever felt totally alone, totally lonesome?" He was speaking from his heart, a heart that was aching. "I thought it was bad in prison, but this, this is like prison. My body is free, but not my mind. Do you have any idea what I'm trying to say?" Then he laughed a little, "I need to snap out of this so I can help my brother."

Athena recalled how bereft she had been when her husband died. She understood James's pain, and felt for him even more. And unless she had lost the ability to read men, James was feeling something too. Focus, she thought, you're writing a book, remember your aesthetic distance. "Is there anything I can do for you?" Athena asked.

"Would you like to go get a cup of coffee or something?" James asked.

"Sure, but would you mind if we went to Vista? It's only a few miles north of here." Citrus City was small enough that tongues would wag if she and James showed up at Captain Kidd's or one of the local places, she thought.

I would go anywhere with you, he thought. "OK, sure, I'll follow you in my car."

When they reached the mall, they parked side by side, and walked to the small café inside.

"We can sit and I can connect to Wi-Fi," she told him.

"To what?" James asked. "Don't go getting all science fiction on me."

She laughed. "No, it's my tablet. At Beth's house I pulled up the church area on Google and saw a few interesting things I'd like to show you."

She had his attention now.

"I have no idea what you're talking about. You say you can see maps, local maps on your computer?"

"Yes, here, I'll show you. Sit beside me."

James sat. Oh no I can't sit here, this is way too close to her, he thought. Her perfume is getting to me;

it's taking over my body. I can't concentrate on a word she's saying. If I close my eyes—

"Uh, what were you saying?"

"Concentrate, James," she said with a smile. Damn he looks good when he's happy, she thought. "When I pull this up, you can see the church, cemetery and all. But look here, it's the trailer park and a road leading right up to the back of the Parnell ranch. It looks like a back entrance." She looked at James to make sure he was looking at the map.

He could see as a crow would see, looking down on what appeared to be the graveyard. Nearby was a trailer park, and running past it was an undefined road or path wide enough for a car, leading to the Parnell property where his brother was killed.

"I wonder if anyone there uses it?" he said. "If there are kids there, I would bet they would know all about it," he added, thinking of his own childhood.

"When I showed this to Beth she wasn't surprised," Athena continued. "Her son Taylor and some of his friends slipped in there to have beer parties a couple times. I don't think the sheriff knows about it, he is from a different generation. He doesn't have kids, so he doesn't get the underage party info." Athena laughed. "Beth told Taylor if it happened again, he would lose his car and have to ride the bus to school for the rest of the year. That's a fate worse than death for a teenage boy. He never did it again."

James laughed. "I stop by the sheriff's office every day," he said. "Tomorrow I'm going to mention this to Keenan. I'm also going to tell him it came from you."

"I don't know if that's smart! Sheriff Long said for us to butt out, remember?"

James remembered, and he planned to say something about that, too. But those matters could wait.

"I'm not trying to change the subject," he said, "but would you like to join me again for a cup of coffee or something sometime soon, maybe at Captain's?"

"I'd like that," Athena said, and James's spirits soared.

CHAPTER 11: Monday, November 15

The next morning found James in his usual place. Since he had no job, he made it his business every day to stop in the sheriff's office. He was glad he could talk to Deputy McDuff, even though he wasn't happy with Sheriff Long. It hurt him to think someone in his position hadn't done more about his brother.

"Good morning," James said.

"Hi James, how are you today?" Keenan said. He was almost horizontal in his chair, his feet up on his desk, reclining back so far James was amazed he didn't tumble over. Sheriff Long grunted and continued drinking his coffee. "Take a load off," Keenan said, motioning James to sit.

James parked his body in the chair by Keenan's desk.

"What's on your mind today, something working in that brain of yours?"

"Hey guys, do you think Shorty would hire me? I'm headed over there, I could use a reference."

"If he can't, he'll know who can," Keenan said. "Give him a shot."

"Sure thing," Sheriff Long said. "Tell him I'll put in a good word for you, son."

James lingered at Keenan's desk. "Um, there's something I came up with yesterday that I think you should know about," he said.

Keenan pulled his legs up off the desk and leaned forward as his chair snapped back into a seating position. "What you got, hoss?" he said, humoring James.

"Well, remember you said that no one saw anything suspicious or anyone leaving the Parnell property the day my brother was…" James found it hard to say the word.

Keenan felt for him. "Yeah, we didn't find any eyewitnesses who saw any unusual activity that day," he said, lapsing into cop-speak to smooth over the awkward moment. "If we had, we would have been on it."

"Well, did you know there's a back way onto the property?' James said.

"Say what?" Keenan asked. Now he was all ears. Sheriff Long put down the *Playboy* magazine he had been ogling and perked up an ear.

"That's right," James said. "Matter of fact, if you turn on your computer, I'll show it to you." Computers were one more thing James had missed during his years in prison, but Athena had been a good teacher. She had showed him how to use Google Earth to find just about anywhere on line. As Keenan booted up his PC, James added, "Now just go to Google Earth and put in the name of the ranch and Citrus City."

Keenan followed the directions.

"Now zoom out," James said, as he came around the desk and stood behind Keenan.

"Well, I'll be dammed," Keenan said, as the satellite image clearly showed the trail connecting the trailer park with the ranch.

"I'll be double-damned," Sheriff Long said, as he joined James at Keenan's desk. The three men were transfixed looking at the map. Each one was looking at something different.

"Yup, there's the road," Keenan said

"There's the cemetery," James said.

"And there's the trailer park," the sheriff added. "Boy, you acting like some kind of detective. How'd you figure that out?"

James blushed. "Well, I had some help. Uh, you know Athena, Beth Filmore's sister?"

"That nosy broad?" Sheriff Long said.

"She's not—I mean, she's just trying to help," James said. He had to control his temper. He was surprised at how he reacted to the sheriff's putdown of Athena. "She met me at the cemetery Sunday; I had gone out there to talk to Frank, and she had one of those tablets. She was able to bring this up on her screen."

"Well, I'll be," Sheriff Long said.

James looked at Long, not sure how to word what he wanted to say next. But he knew it had to be said. Beth and Athena were two of the smartest women he knew, and it wasn't right that they had to sneak around to help.

"Sheriff, Athena told me you had visited her and Beth and asked them to stay out of the case," he blurted out.

"You did what?" Keenan asked, turning to confront his boss.

The sheriff pulled out his big white handkerchief. "Well, I think—well we might be—aw hell, what I'm saying is, I told those two meddling broads to let us do our job, let us handle this. I thought they were just muddying up the water." Mopping the sweat from his face, he added, "Maybe I was wrong. Sorry."

If looks could kill, the sheriff would be a goner and Keenan would be facing Death Row.

"What did you do that for?" Keenan snapped.

James was trying hard to look serious, but the sheriff looked like a kid with his hand in the cookie jar and he liked it. Served him right.

"Beth's sister is from Chicago and thinks we are a bunch of bumpkins," the sheriff blustered. "We don't need her watching over our shoulder."

"No, she doesn't," James blurted out. "She wants to help and I think she can, she's very smart."

Keenan eyed James, whose face turned red as he looked away fast.

"OK, Sheriff, we can use all the help we can get," Keenan said. "Let's tell the women it was just a misunderstanding and go from there."

"Yeah," the sheriff answered. "Maybe I let my personal feelings dictate my decision. Should I call them?"

Keenan was thinking and his blue eyes were twinkling as he did the math. "No, we can let James do it." Looking at James he said, "That should be worth a few points, if you get my drift."

James's brow furrowed briefly, then he smiled when he saw the light.

"Yeah, I do. Thanks."

"OK, that's settled. James, why don't you head over to Shorty's before the rush and ask him about that job?"

James didn't need a second invitation; he made his goodbyes and took off.

"So what's next?' Sheriff Long asked.

"We're bringing Jake, Frankie's friend, in for some more questioning tomorrow. Then I'm going out to the trailer park," Keenan said, checking his notes and calendar. "Sheriff, remember Matt Philips? He's on probation and he lives in that trailer park we saw on the map. I'm going out there tomorrow and lean on him, maybe he'll remember something about an SUV. As Churchill said, this may not be the beginning of the end, but it's the end of the beginning."

"What?" Sheriff Long said. "There you go with that Churchill crap again."

CHAPTER 12: Tuesday, November 16

The drive to the office was short, but it gave Sheriff Long time to think, alone, without the input of a know-it-all deputy. He had done his job long before Keenan McDuff appeared, and he would get things back under control. If there was anything he didn't like, it was not being in charge. His office, his rules. But he had pushed this case on Keenan, now he would let him run with it.

He arrived at the office well before his normal time. Everything was set for their interview. Keenan had found Jake with no problem. He had moved about twenty miles away and was living with an old girlfriend. The difficulty was in convincing Jake to open up old wounds.

There wouldn't be any good cop, bad cop tactics. Jake wasn't a suspect, and had never been. Jake was a young man who had lost his best friend. He was their last chance to find out if Frank had been up to something. They did, however, need to jog his memory about the morning when he found Frank and his family. It was going to be tough on him. Jake had definitely been traumatized by the experience. They would need to make him reach deep inside his mind, go places he never wanted to go again. It was their last chance.

Deputy Wiley was in on time. "You two look like you are preparing for something big, what's happening?" he asked, sitting down to have his coffee.

"Jake Wells is due here soon," Sheriff Long replied. "We're re-interviewing him."

"I thought he told us all he knew five years ago," Wiley said.

"Yeah, he probably did," the sheriff said, cutting his eyes toward Keenan. "But, we're doing it again." He changed the subject. "What's happening on the road?"

"Nothing much," Wiley frowned, "It's hard to get in and out of the café lately. Everybody and his brother asking questions."

Sheriff Long thought for a minute. "Wiley, why don't you take road patrol today, keep your eyes and ears open and let us know what you hear, okay?"

"Sure chief," Wiley said as he began gathering his stuff. He knew the sheriff and Keenan were up to something and he resented it.

"I'll just get out of here—you guys'll be busy, see ya at five." And he was gone.

"Keenan, before Jake gets here, talk to me," the sheriff said, without a second thought for his frustrated deputy. "Our records show you were playing that guitar of yours at Captain's that night and Jake was there late. Tell me about it, all you remember, and I'll record it this time."

Keenan smiled. Who said you can't teach an old dog new tricks?

"I've been thinking about that night a lot." Keenan said. "I know how hard it is to recall a snapshot in time from your past. This was five years ago. This was big." Keenan relaxed, let out a sigh and started. "I was playing that night. Jake was there," he paused. "He is a very low key kind of guy. He was talking to a few friends, they were sitting at a table near the band, he danced a little, but mostly the guys were drinking and talking. My night was uneventful. Captain's was busy and the night was young, so the Captain was happy. But then it started to rain just before we started playing. Captain wasn't happy about that. It rained for about an hour or so. It was more than just rain, it was a storm. Lots of thunder and lightning. We never lost power but it was still storming when the set ended."

Long was listening to Keenan retell the story of the night Frank Jenkins was killed, the night that changed the town forever. No one blamed him for not solving the crime, his own conscience did that. But people no longer left their doors unlocked and no longer looked at strangers the way they did before the murders.

Now the pressure was high. The town was buzzing. It wasn't possible to pop into the café for a cup of coffee without Lola or one of the old guys who held up the lunch counter asking for the latest developments. He was bombarded with questions and he felt obligated to answer as many as he could. Everybody had a tip.

"The night seemed to be a normal night, except for the storm; nothing unusual at the bar," Keenan continued. "No fights. No strangers coming in, just the regulars, everyone having a good time." Keenan paused and looked at his notes. "Let me ask you, Sheriff, what was happening in other parts of town? Did anyone report anything out of the ordinary?"

Long was scanning the report, trying to recall anything about that night.

"No, not really, just a couple that had parked at the 7-11 waiting out the storm. They saw a dark SUV go by. It caught their eye because it was the only car on the road. But it was raining pretty hard and they said the windows were tinted. And they thought it had out-of-state plates. It was headed west on 2nd street and turned north at 41, going out of town. .We didn't have much to follow-up with. No one else remembered the car."

"If it was headed west, that means it came from the east; it had to have passed Riverview Mobile Home Park" Keenan said. "Did you interview anyone from there? Maybe someone saw it. Or maybe, the driver was visiting someone in the park."

"No, we didn't interview anyone else about the SUV that I recall."

Keenan made a note in his notebook. "Well, it's time for Jake to be here. I hope he's not late," Keenan added, looking out the window.

Both men were watching as Jake opened the door, hesitated, then walked in.

His hair was graying at the temples, giving him a premature aged look that wasn't flattering. The lines in his face had become more prominent, like those of a man old beyond his years. He even walked like an old man; kind of shuffling.

"Hey Jake, good to see you," Sheriff Long extended his hand.

Jake shook his hand. "Hey Sheriff," and looked at Keenan. "Hey man, good to see you."

"I haven't seen you at Captain's in a while," Keenan said.

"I know. I haven't been there in a while," he replied. "Let's get this over with, I gotta get to work soon, and this is the last place I want to be."

"OK, Jake," Keenan said, leading the way to the conference room. "Let's do it in here; we're already set up for you."

"Keenan, that was the worst day of my life," Jake replied. "I've moved on but it's still there. It still haunts me. Frankie and I were best friends."

Keenan said, "Jake, let me say I'm very sorry you have to go through this, not once but twice. Frank was your best friend. And as hard as this is, I know you would like to see justice for him and his family. So I'll make this as painless as possible. OK, are you ready?"

They sat around the conference table, got the recorder going, and then Sheriff Long stated the date and the names of the three men in the room. "Now Jake, I'm going to record this, hope you don't mind? This shouldn't take long."

"Yeah, I'm as ready as I can get, so get on with it," Jake said.

"First, I'll ask you to tell us in your own words about that morning; then we have a few questions," Keenan said.

Jake nodded his head.

"Please speak up, for the recorder," the sheriff prodded

"OK," Jake said, closing his eyes for just a moment. "This is almost as hard now as it was five years ago. But I'll try." And then he began.

"It was still dark when I drove up; the lights were on in the house. I walked to the front door. I always knocked first and then I walked in." Jake was visibly shaking. "I need a minute." After a short pause he continued "I called Frankie, not too loud, didn't want to wake the kids. I got no answer. There were mud tracks on the living room floor. I called a little louder and started toward the kitchen, which is in the back of the house. I had to pass the bedroom."

The only sound in the room, other than Jake's tortured voice, was the whining of the tape recorder.

"Oh my God, this is hard, I can't do this. Why did this happen?" He took a deep breath, closed his eyes, opened them, and started again. "I had to pass the bedroom, I glanced in. All I could see was blood; then I saw Cary, laying there naked with blood all over the place—Oh Lord," he wailed. "I turned and ran out the door. I started throwing up the minute I was outside. I wasn't thinking, I jumped in my truck; then I thought I needed to call for help."

He paused again, this time he wiped his eyes on his sleeve. "I drove to the Mobil station on US 41. I used the pay phone there. I waited until I saw you and the deputies and then I followed you back there."

"Good, Jake, take a breather," Long said. "You're doing fine. We have a few questions, like I said. And then you can go."

Keenan paused. Jake swallowed a few times, ran his hands through his thinning air, and then sat up straight. Keenan glanced at his notes. "Did Frank have any enemies?"

"No, none," Jake said. "If he had I would have known about them. He was my best friend, we shared everything."

"Any problems, at home, say with his wife or maybe a jealous boyfriend anything like that?"

"No, he and Cary got along fine, she was a little mad at him about our fishing trip. She wanted to go shopping that day. He said she would get over it. He was going to buy her a ring for Christmas, one she saw last year and he couldn't afford. But this year he had the money."

"Where was the money coming from?" Keenan asked

"Well," Jake paused. "Well, he told me he had a few dollars saved." The look on his face told them that Jake wouldn't make a good poker player. Long and Keenan both knew Jake was holding something back.

"Did he say how he saved the money?"

"He asked me not to tell, he didn't want his boss to find out. He was afraid he would lose his job. I promised."

"OK, but that's all in the past, Frank can't lose his job now, can he?" Keenan leaned over the table and said, "This would be a good time to say what's on your mind."

Jake's face was red and he wouldn't look them in the eye. He didn't want to tell Frankie's secret. Not even now.

"I only know what Frankie told me," Jake said stubbornly.

"And what was that?" Sheriff Long snapped; he was getting impatient. Keenan shot him a look, then turned back to Jake. "Take your time."

"Frankie said he came across some hunters a few days before," Jake said. The words rushed out; Jake had been holding them back for years. He seemed relieved to tell the rest of the story.

"They were hunting on the ranch and he told them it was private property. They offered him $300 if he would let them stay a little while. No one would know. He took the money and left. Later he was real worried Mr. Parnell would find out and fire him."

"Jake, you did very well today. Thanks a lot for your help. A couple more questions and then you can go." Keenan continued. Now this was something new. He was excited, but tried to keep his voice steady. "Did Frank say what area they were hunting in? It might be important. That ranch is 4,000 acres and covers a lot of woods and pasture."

Jake was feeling a little better about the conversation; but he still wanted this to be over. He glanced at his watch.

"Yeah, it was by the old grove of trees just east of the big pond. I know exactly where it is."

"If we need you to find it, could you? Do you think you could help us, just for Frankie?"

"I haven't been in that area in five years, but yes, I'll do it for Frankie." Jake said. He put his head in his hands and his narrow shoulders were shaking. He was crying.

"Just a little bit more, and then we're done. Did he tell you what these guys looked like?" Keenan asked, almost holding his breath.

"Yeah, he said they sure didn't look like hunters. There were three of them. He said the one with the most tattoos did all the talking. He said he had never seen tats like that before, not that he had seen a lot, but they kinda scared him."

"Could you draw a picture of what the tattoos looked like?" Keenan asked, producing a piece of paper.

"I think so. Frankie said one was real creepy—it was on the guy's neck. Can you imagine, getting tattoos on your neck? He had some on his hands too. HATE and LOVE were written on his fingers."

Jake drew pictures of the tattoo on the man's neck. It was a half moon with a devil's face. "This is just the way Frankie said it looked."

They had about all they were going to get from Jake. As he shambled out of the office, tears were rolling down his cheeks. Jake looked back at the sheriff and deputy as he left. "Frankie deserves justice," he said as he slammed the door shut.

Inside the office, Long and McDuff were already adding this new information to the evidence board. It was new, but was it of any significance? The gears were rolling in Keenan's mind. "Let's find the couple that saw the SUV," he said. "Maybe they'll remember something else. Nothing is too small to check out."

At last they had a new clue, something that had been missing the last five years. There was a glimmer of hope in Keenan's eyes. He knew where to go from here.

CHAPTER 13: Wednesday, November 17

Keenan looked at the dry-erase board, he looked at the cork board, and he looked at a fly taking a break on the wall. Things were hopping. He sat down, put his feet up on the desk, and thought about how fast things had changed. He had taken the job to be closer to home, but after the hectic pace of life as a road deputy in Tampa, Citrus City had turned out to be Boresville. He had actually considered leaving the force.

And then James Jenkins came to town and everything changed. Keenan knew that solving the case would be a matter of hard work and luck. Speaking of hard work, he was about to try and change his luck.

"Sheriff, I'm taking a trip out to the mobile home park," he said. "You're more familiar with those people; they've lived there for years; you mind taking a ride with me?"

"Well, I don't know, Keenan," Sheriff Long replied. November in Florida could get pretty hot, and the sheriff knew they'd be getting out and walking door to door in the old trailer park right when the sun was at its highest. "What do you think we could find out there?"

"Well, if the SUV came from that way, maybe the occupants were visiting someone; if they were, we'll find out who and why, maybe. Besides, you're sitting too much, get out, move," Keenan laughed. "Walk off that last donut you had for breakfast."

As if on cue, Deputy Wiley walked in, carrying a greasy bag of donuts from the café. Sheriff Long and Keenan both burst out laughing.

"What—what's the joke?" Wiley asked as he made his way to his desk.

"It's just the donuts, son, nothing personal," Sheriff Long said. "Well, now that you put it like that," he said to Keenan, "let's roll. Wiley, we're headed out to check on a lead in that Jenkins murder. You mind holding down the fort?"

"10-4, boss," Wiley said as he ripped open the bag of donuts.

"Whew," said the sheriff, as they left the air-conditioned office for the bright glare and humid temperature of the street. "OK, mind if I drive?"

"No problem," Keenan said. "I can go over these notes on the way."

As the men drove past Shorty's, the proprietor waved.

"Wonder how James made out ?" Keenan said.

"Aw, I think he'll do fine. Shorty can always use an extra hand. He's had Wiley doing some odd jobs for him for about a year."

Keenan barely heard the sheriff's answer. He had been flipping pages in his notebook.

"Help me out here," he said, half to himself. "Here's the timeline so far: "December 08; Frankie discovers three trespassers on the property. They pay him three hundred dollars to let them hunt there. No one in town can recall three strangers.

"One week later Frankie picks up his bonus check from Mr. Parnell. Someone enters his home and murders his family. He returns and is also murdered. Storms that night. SUV spotted near 7-11, headed out of town.

"Right now it looks like the killers weren't hopped-up or crazy. There were no fingerprints; it looked like they knew what they were doing."

As he spoke, Sheriff Long appeared to have his mind solely on the road. But he was thinking, damn if that Keenan doesn't sound like those guys on CSI.

Gotta give him credit, he's making sure to touch every base.

"Yeah, son, I have to agree with you. No broken locks or windows, so they must have been smooth enough to just walk right up to the front door. Cary must have let them in. Did she know them? Did they threaten her? The kids were getting ready for bed, so I would say it was after 6 p.m."

Keenan was looking at the sheriff, impressed that he was adding something useful to the conversation. "That's about the time Frank left to pick up his bonus check from Parnell," Keenan said. "Were the killers watching the house? Did they know he was leaving? Did they know when he would be back? Let's assume for a minute they did."

"OK, what was the motive?" Sheriff Long asked. Now the men were in rhythm, walking the case back and forth to uncover anything they may have missed. "What was the connection to this family? Why the whole family? Leave no witness? If they only wanted to kill Frankie, they could have done it almost anywhere on the ranch without risk of being seen by the family. This was deliberate, total elimination. We are missing a motive."

"That's right, Sheriff. And when we know this we will be closer to solving it."

"Did this have something to do with the trespassers on the ranch?" Keenan added. "What happened to those men? No one else saw them, but if they were hunters, seems like they would have had a drink at Captain's or stopped somewhere nearby for supplies or food. But no one claims to have seen them before or after the encounter with Frank. Let's assume they could have something to do with this. I don't know how we can identify them, after five years."

Gravel crunched beneath the wheels of the green-and-white as Sheriff Long steered off the blacktop onto a back road. According to the map, the road went nowhere; it ended at the border of the Parnell Ranch. They drove about a quarter mile up the road, then veered left onto a dirt path. On the right was a dilapidated colony of rusted tin and aluminum mobile homes, some listing to one side. A kid's Big Wheel, overflowing trash cans, and junked cars punctuated the depressing landscape.

"Well, we need to move," Keenan said as he got out the car. "Let's start a door-to-door."

Several of the residents at the park were less than law abiding. There had been rumors of meth labs and grow houses out along that road and the trailer park, for some reason, attracted more than its share of ex-cons. They would visit them first, and maybe save themselves valuable time.

Their first stop was the Philips place.

Matt Philips lived with his mother. He was in his early 30s and his mother was on disability. Matt was no stranger to the sheriff's office; he had been in and out of jail so many times he couldn't count that high.

"Anybody home?" Keenan said, as he rapped on the door. No answer. "Anybody home?" he said a little louder. At that point the door opened next door and an old man stuck his head out.

"Keep that up and I'm calling the sheriff," yelled the geezer.

"I am the sheriff, you old duffer," Sheriff Long said. "How you doin', John?

"Hey yourself, Sheriff, what you making so much noise for? I was trying to sleep."

"I'm looking for Matt. Have you seen him?"

"No, and good riddance to bad rubbish."

"What do you mean?" Keenan stepped nearer to John so he wouldn't have to yell.

"This is my deputy, Keenan McDuff," Sheriff Long said.

John wore hearing aids and glasses with magnifiers on them. After the introductions, Keenan stepped up to peek in Matt's trailer.

"Nobody here, looks like they left in a hurry."

"Yeah, I said good riddance," John said again.

"Did you see Matt leave?" the sheriff asked.

"Yeah, about 12 or 1 last night. Why?"

"You saw him leave?" Keenan said.

"You ain't listening," John said. "I said I did."
"You want it in writin'?"

"No, just tell me what you saw," Keenan said.

"Yeah, I got up in the night, you know I have this prostrate thing, you know what I mean?—"

"—You mean prostate," Sheriff Long interrupted.

"No, I mean I got to pee all the time," John snapped. Keenan snickered. "Well, as I was sayin', I saw headlights shining into my place. When I looked out, there was this big black car parked near the door. Matt and his ma were getting in it."

"Did you see Matt after that?" This was like pulling teeth, Keenan thought,

"I'm not that nosy, you know. But I did see him throw some things in the car before they left."

"Did you hear anything? Were they talking? Whose car was it?" Keenan was throwing out questions as fast as he could think.

"I didn't hear a word," John said pointing to his ears. "I don't sleep with my hearing aids in!"

Matt was on probation, Keenan thought; if he was going somewhere he needed to report in way before he left. They hadn't heard a word from the parole and probation office up in Tampa.

"Thanks John, good work. Keep your eyes and ears open. And if he comes back give me a call. Here's my card." Sheriff Long stepped away from John's front door; then thought about something else.

"John," he called, before John could slam his door. "Could I ask you something?"

"You already did. You mean something else? Yeah, go ahead."

"Have you seen any vehicles using that gate over there?"

"Not in a while, why?"

"When was the last time you saw someone there?"

"Well, let me think, my memory isn't what it used to be, I can't remember everything like I used to." John was thinking.

This will take a while, Keenan thought to himself.

"It's been a long time, maybe a month or two, maybe a year. I'm not sure."

"Can you describe the vehicle or person that was there?"

"Hell no, I can't really see—not good anyway. I think these glasses are too old, they don't work good anymore. I couldn't even tell what kind of car was here last night."

"OK, call us if Matt comes home or if you see anyone by the gate."

"Sure, and good to see you guys—just don't make so much noise the next time you come out here," John said as he slammed his door.

"Sheriff, did you mention to anyone that we would be going to the trailer park today?" Keenan asked.

"No, did you?"

"No." Keenan thought for a moment, and then made up his mind. "We need to take a visit out to the ranch's back entrance," he said. "What do you say?"

"We can't just trespass, if Parnell finds out—" The sheriff couldn't even finish the sentence.

"If anything comes up, we'll say, someone reported a homeless camp out there."

The sheriff didn't budge.

"Look, you stay here, I'm going, you are so worried about Parnell—"

"Wait a minute," Sheriff Long started to move. "I'll go; I've got to see this for myself."

The distance from the trailer park to the ranch could have been walked by an ambitious person. But in the heat, both men voted to cruise up in the green-and-white. They got out of the car, stood, and looked around. East was just woods, west was the park with several seedy residences within shouting distance. South was a rusty gate, in the middle of a barbed wire fence. The gate was old and beaten down, but the lock was brand new. Keenan touched it and then brought his fingertip up to his nose. "Yeah, WD 40," he said to the sheriff. His mind was in full gear.

Looking past the gate he could see a visible road in the tall grass. He took pictures with his phone for his records.

"Let's take a look," Keenan. He popped the trunk and took out a pair of bolt cutters; he had the lock off before the sheriff knew what he was doing.

"My God, boy," the sheriff said, looking in all directions.

"Well, it doesn't look like anyone has been here in a while. Let's see how far we can drive, before we have to walk. We really need a four-wheeler."

When they went as far as the car could go, they stopped at a stand of trees, where the car would be hidden from view.

"We can walk from here," Keenan said as he took out his phone and started taking pictures. "I want to see the area Jake mentioned. Can you walk that far, old man?"

"Yeah, I'm not as old as you might think!"

"The pond must be this way," Keenan said leading the way.

They stopped and looked for the pond, but with the dry season, it was much smaller than expected. The high shoulders of the banks showed how far the water had receded. Reeds and cattails were covering most of the surface. Everywhere they looked the ground was rooted up by wild boars. Keenan took more pictures.

"It's almost impossible to determine exactly where they were," Sheriff Long said, studying the ground.

Keenan suddenly had a feeling they were in the right place. "Look at that!" he exclaimed. "What is that sticking out of the ground?"

"Where? All I see is plowed-up dirt from the wild pigs."

"Yeah, that's what I'm looking at," Keenan said squatting down and pulling an object out of the ground. "Oh my God! It's a bone, I think it's a leg bone."

Sheriff Long gasped. Keenan was holding what appeared to be a femur.

"Put that down, son, put it back," the sheriff said sharply, mindful that they were trespassing. "But take a few pictures first."

He looked around. Suddenly he saw several depressions in the earth around the area. The dry season had leached moisture out of the soil, causing any freshly turned ground to sink. The depressions, he knew, were probably filled-in holes. Based on what they had just found, that could only mean one thing.

"Son," Sheriff Long said slowly, "I think we're on to something bad. Let's head on back to the trailer park and do some more door to door."

Keenan knew when to mouth off and when to shut up. "Sure, Sheriff," he said, gently placing the bone on the ground. He took a few more photographs. Then the two men, chastened by what they had seen, headed back to the cruiser.

* * *

Hours later, as the long shadows of a November twilight descended, Long and Keenan decided to call it quits. They had canvassed the whole park and had come up empty. The adrenaline raised by the discovery of the bone had faded, but they knew that they were on to something.

"Come on, son," Sheriff Long said. "I know when I'm licked." They began trudging back to the car. In a lot of ways, Keenan reminded Long of Martin. Both were smart, educated, and hardworking. Despite his reservations, he knew he'd have to follow Keenan's lead and give Parnell a call. He still had his doubts about Keenan—the boy was pushy and he acted like a know-it-all. But failing to solve the Jenkins murders was like a hole in his gut. Now the kid appeared to be moving the case forward. For the first time, he was glad Keenan was on board.

"Sheriff, sheriff," Keenan said, touching his arm.

"Oh, sorry, I guess my mind was miles away," he answered, with a sheepish grin on his face. "Boy, let me tell you something," Sheriff Long said. "I don't know why you do half the things you do, but thanks to you, I think we're on to something."

Kennan looked over at the older man. He supposed that was the closest thing to praise he'd get from a man who'd barely tolerated him before.

"Sheriff, how hard will it be to get a search warrant for the Parnell property?" he asked.

"The problem is the man who owns the property, Mr. Cleveland Parnell the sheriff answered.

"You think he'll let us search without a warrant?" Keenan asked.

"When fat pigs fly," Long said. The last thing he wanted to do was approach Parnell again. He took out a large white handkerchief and mopped the sweat running down his face.

"Let's call it quits for the day, but I want us to get a jump start tomorrow. It's too late to get to the courthouse for a warrant, but we'll get on that tomorrow. Them bones ain't going nowhere,"

CHAPTER 14: Thursday, November 18

James was feeling better about Citrus City. He had met a nice lady, Deputy McDuff seemed to have accepted him, and people generally seemed to be friendly. He didn't know if he would ever find out what happened to his family, but he had the satisfaction of working hard to find out. If he could find a job he would feel much better.

"Hi Shorty," James said.

"Well if it isn't the man rattling cages!" Shorty said. "You been shaking up this little town of ours." He moved his cigar to the other side of his mouth, then put an arm around James's shoulder and pulled him in close. "What has old Sheriff Long come up with? What's the latest on the case?"

Shorty seemed so friendly that James was about to tell him everything he knew. But a sixth sense stopped him. Besides, that wasn't what he was there about.

"Well, Shorty, they don't tell me much about law enforcement business, just that they're still working on it," James said. "But that's not what I'm here about."

Shorty pulled away. "Now this isn't about that creampuff I sold you, now is it? You remember, that sale was 'as is.'"

James smiled. "No, the car's running fine."

Shorty calmed down. "That's right; you buy a car from Shorty, you'll be able to pass it on to your grandkids."

"Shorty, I'm here because I need a job," James said in a nervous rush. "I'm a hard worker, you know a little of my past and the sheriff will vouch for me. I'm willing to do whatever you need me to do."

Shorty looked hard at James. This might work out, he thought.

"OK, I'll give you a chance," Shorty said. "I can use a detail man, washing, waxing, cleaning, and moving cars around. How does that sound? The pay isn't much, but it's better than nothing."

"Are you saying you'll give me the job?" James was grinning from ear to ear. His first job since he got out of prison.

"We transport cars in and out of Tampa," Shorty said. "I have another car lot there. Tom Wiley works part-time for me. You probably met him; he's a deputy in Sheriff Long's office."

"Yes, I did meet him. Nice guy," James said. "Most of the people I've met here are nice. This seems like a great little town."

"You can start this afternoon. We'll put you on part-time, from 1 to 4. Be here at 1 and I'll get you going."

James was walking on clouds when he left. He needed to tell someone, and he knew just the one.

He pulled out his phone and as he punched in a number his heart was fluttering.

"Hello," Athena answered.

"Hi Athena, guess what? I just got a job," James said.

"That's great, where?" Athena asked. She sounded flustered.

"I'll be working at Shorty's. It's a no brainer, but at least I'm working."

"Great, let's celebrate. What do you say? My treat," Athena suggested.

"OK," James said.

"Good, I'm helping Beth put a perm in, so I've got to go. I'll call you back and we can decide when and where tonight. See you," and she was gone.

He drove back to the Days Inn to get cleaned up for work. He had just taken a shower a few hours ago, but he wanted to change his clothes for the job.

Just as he entered his room, the motel phone on the nightstand next to his bed rang.

Who could be calling me on that phone? Maybe it's Athena.

"Hello."

"James Jenkins?"

"Yes."

"This is Ron Johnson; I'm calling from the Tampa office of the state parole and probation office."

James felt a chill go through him. What had he done now?

"Mr. Jenkins, apparently your paperwork has been fouled up. We just now found out where you were—do you know you're supposed to be reporting once a week to your probation officer?"

James thought for a moment. "No, sir," he answered. "Mr. Graham, the superintendent, said they'd forward all my material here, and told me a parole officer would be contacting me."

"Well, I hate to say it, but unless I see you soon, you'll be in non-compliance," Johnson answered.

"What does that mean, sir?" James asked. He knew what it meant.

"You could be back in Florida State, and I don't mean the university," Johnson said with a laugh. "Sorry, that's Parole and Probation department humor."

James didn't laugh.

After an awkward moment, Johnson said, "Look, it appears the mistake was ours. Any chance of you getting up here sometime today? I'll process you, backdate the information, and you'll be good to go."

"I just started a new job," James said.

"That's good, that's real good," Johnson said. "But we've got to get you processed." There was a pause. "Look, what time do you get off from work?

"4 o'clock."

"Well, today's Thursday, it's my night shift day. Could you get up here by, say, 6?"

Oh no, James thought, there goes my date with Athena. But there won't be a date with anybody unless I get this straight.

"Yes, sir," he told Johnson. "Um, could you give me the address, please?"

Johnson gave him directions and the address to the office.

"See you at 6," he said, then hung up.

Damn, James though. I guess I'll have to cancel. He called Athena's number, but it just rang. He looked at the clock. It was 12:30, just enough time for a shower and a trip back to Shorty's.

* * *.

James was on time at the car lot. Shorty was waiting for him.

"OK, let me walk you through this here place," he said. Shorty had a big lot full of cars in various colors, makes, and models. But he steered James toward the back, where a huge metal building housed even more rows of cars.

"This here is where you'll be doing most of your work," Shorty said. "Now each car will have a number; you need to make sure that car is placed where its number is marked on the parking space in here—you got that?"

Does he think I'm stupid? James thought. But a job was a job, so he just nodded, smiled, and said yes sir.

"Now say I have number 7 here, where would you park it?"

"In number 7 spot, sir," James said, feeling like an idiot.

"That's right, boy, that's right—you catch on real good," Shorty said. "Now you'll be detailing each of these babies, sprucing them up and making them look as good as that piece of road candy I sold you, right?"

"Yes, sir," James said again.

"Just make sure the car numbers agree with the numbers on the paperwork and with the parking spaces," Shorty said "You think that'll be a problem?"

"I think I've got it," James answered, looking around. "Where's the mechanic?"

"He comes in at night, this is his part-time job," Shorty said breezily. "Don't worry about him, you'll be gone when he comes in."

Shorty started to walk back to his office. "When you're done, check in with me, then you're through for the day."

James looked at the paperwork and picked out a car. All the cars were in great shape, he just needed to spruce them up. Piece of cake. By the second car he noticed that they all had been tampered with. The door panels were loose and there were gouge marks around the screws that held them in place. Nothing on the paperwork noted that type of work, but he could tell something had been changed. By the third car he was beginning to think that the mechanic was making repairs and not noting them on the work order; probably not legal. But who was he to question it? Used car dealers got a bad rap, and it was usually deserved. He had a job, that's all that mattered.

Cleaning up for the day, he took his wet rags and buffing cloths in the back to throw them in the bin. He marveled again at the size of the building. What a big garage, he thought, there were several cars inside waiting for the mechanic. Shorty did a lot of business here.

I wonder if the mechanic could use some help, he thought. I used to fix my mother's car; also, the pay would be better.

That's when he noticed the surveillance cameras. They seemed to be everywhere. And those were just the ones he could see. Shorty doesn't trust anyone, he thought. Oh well, I'm out of here.

He walked to the office and Shorty was waiting for him.

"Here's your time card," he said. "How was it today? Think you can do this?"

"Oh yeah," James answered. "Thanks again for the job, Shorty, I'll see you tomorrow."

* * *

Tom Wiley had worked a full shift at the sheriff's department; but he wasn't tired. Far from it; he was rejuvenated. Working in the sheriff's office gave him a feeling of giving back to his community. His part-time job allowed him some freedom not possible in a small town. He took a fast shower, changed clothes, and headed out to exercise that freedom tonight.

At Shorty's, the auto transport carrier was ready to be loaded.

"Hey Tom," Shorty said.

It was six and starting to get dark, but Wiley had no trouble loading the transport by himself; he had been doing this for a year. The pay was good and it allowed him the excuse to travel to Tampa two or three times a week. What he did in Tampa wasn't anyone's business, except maybe Shorty's.

"Shorty, how are you? Wiley answered.

"I want you to know, I hired that Jenkins boy to do the detailing," Shorty said. "Let me know if he screws up the parking spaces."

"What are his hours? Where is he?"

"He's gone for the day already. He'll work 1 to 4. So he'll be long gone when you and the mechanic come in."

Wiley had misgivings about Jenkins, but he only worked for Shorty, and Shorty didn't really ask his opinion on anything.

"You going to see mama tonight?" asked Shorty, pushing his face up close to Wiley's and leering.

"I'm not sure yet," Wiley answered, ducking his head. Some day he'll get his, he thought. "Right now I had better get busy."

Before 7 the transport was loaded and ready to roll.

Tom hit the horn twice. Shorty picked up the phone and dialed a number. "He's on his way, have someone there to unload."

Shorty locked the office and walked out the front door just as Rod, the mechanic, was parking at the garage.

"Hey Rod, how's it going?" Shorty yelled.

"Fine, I'll check the inventory again, but I think I have four for tonight," Rod replied.

"Good deal, see you tomorrow," Shorty said, waving.

The transport wasn't the most comfortable ride, but Tom wasn't thinking about the journey, just the destination.

He dropped the transport off at Tampa lot #2 and found the vehicle that had been left for him to return home in.

"OK," he said out loud, "it should be a good night, after all." He checked his appearance in the rear view mirror. "Not bad."

The ride to see mama, as Shorty called Tom's friend, was short. He parked in the driveway of the small bungalow, exited the car, and walked swiftly to the door.

The door opened immediately, "Right on time," Alex said. "I like that. I have a drink waiting for you."

"Thanks, it's been a long day." Tom replied.

Tom put his arms around Alex and gave him a kiss. As he closed the door behind him, he said, "The drink can wait."

* * *

"Damn, her phone is busy; I should have called her earlier," James said. Driving and using a cell phone were not two things he should be doing at the same time. "This is an emergency, officer," he said out loud, laughing as he rehearsed his excuse if Tom or Keenan pulled him over. "Still busy, who could she be talking to?" He wasn't laughing now.

He pulled into the parking lot at Days Inn and there she was. His heart skipped a beat. He parked and jumped out.

"I was just trying to call you," he said to Athena.

"I was trying to call you, too," Athena said with a wide grin on her face. "I didn't know where to meet you."

She came here to meet me, he thought, WOW. I like it.

"Look, I have some bad news for you," he said.

Oh God, Athena thought, is he dumping me before we even go on our first date?

"Um, I don't know how to say this, but I have to go see my parole officer tonight," James said, ducking his head in embarrassment. "It looks like they screwed up the paperwork and I have to see him today or else."

Athena didn't want to hear what "Or else" meant. But spending a few hours visiting a guy's probation officer wasn't her idea of an evening out. The news brought back all of her reservations about having any more to do with James Jenkins beyond business.

He was a remarkable source, an open and honest man who answered her every question about life behind bars and his efforts to find his brother's killers. But still, he was a convict and a professional car detailer. She looked up at him, leaning against her driver's side window, to tell him to forget it.

His deep blue eyes looked back at her.

"Well, we could still get together if you'd like," she heard herself saying. "I heard they have some great restaurants in Tampa. Mind if I drive?"

James couldn't believe it. She didn't put him off after he mentioned the parole officer.

"Would you mind if I run upstairs, for a minute? It will only take a minute, I promise."

"Go ahead, take your time," she replied.

As soon as the elevator door closed, he thought, I should have invited her up here to wait—no, not up here, maybe, oh my God, I don't know. I'll just hurry up.

Her mind raced as she questioned conflicting emotions. What am I doing with this loser? But he's kind, he's caring. She recalled Beth's warnings. Am I really turning into a cougar, am I stalking James because I'm a horny older woman? What happened to using him just for research, nothing else?

It didn't take long for him to change his shirt, comb his hair, and rush back in the parking lot. "I should have asked you if you wanted to come up, I'm sorry," James said, interrupting her train of thought as he leaned in the passenger's window. "Do you need to come up for anything, before we leave?"

What would I want in your room except you? Athena thought. Where'd that come from? "No, I'm fine," she said. "You know, I hear there's a part of Tampa called Ybor City where they have some great restaurants. "I've been meaning to get up there—this was meant to happen."

And how, James thought as he got in and buckled up.

"I've never been to a parole office," she said, laughing nervously.

"This is my first time, too," he said. "And I'm not sure what to expect. They told me it was painless, I'll have to see for myself."

"You just need to check in, right?"

"I think so, give them my address and new job info and get my schedule for future check-ins. And, thanks again for coming, you are a good sport."

"Well it gets me out of Beth's hair for awhile," Athena said, and laughed at her own joke. They started talking about the case, interrupting each other in their excitement at being alone together. In no time at all, James was reading off the directions as they negotiated the streets of Tampa.

As they pulled into the lot near the courthouse, it was almost empty, as the courthouse was closed. The probation office was across the street.

"OK, this shouldn't take long. I hate for you to wait in the car," James said. "Come on and wait inside, it's going to be dark soon."

The office was small, but there were several people ahead of him. James signed his name on a sheet of paper on a desk, then he and Athena took a seat. There were plenty of magazines and books to read on a small table near the seats.

"James Jenkins?" a young-looking officer called.

"Yes, that's me," James said.

"Come on in."

James smiled at Athena. "Here I go."

He then followed the officer through the open door.

As Athena picked up a magazine to read, she noted something familiar.

"I'll be darned," she said out loud, picking up a hardcover book from the table.

There it was; her latest book, *Making Happy*.

She looked around and didn't see any kids, but she guessed some parolee brought her children with her for her appointment.

A short time later, James walked out of the inner office with the officer. "Good luck, James, see you in a couple weeks," he said.

James smiled when he saw Athena.

"Sorry it took so long," he said. "I thought he just needed my address and job info but it was a first interview. I had to read the rules, sign some papers, and a couple other things."

His eyes came to rest on the book she was holding, *Making Happy* by Athena Sands. He took it from her, looked at her, and turned it over. There was a beautiful picture of the woman sitting there watching him.

"Athena, that's you!" he exclaimed as he read the blurb on the back cover. "You won awards for your books, you've written over fifteen books for kids. Wow!"

"Yeah, it is," she said.

"Let's go," he turned and abruptly started walking to the door.

He didn't say a word until they were in the car.

"You didn't tell me you were a writer." He seemed put off by the information.

"There's something wrong with being a writer?" she asked.

"No, nothing," he paused. "When were you going to tell me?"

"You're acting like this is some undercover job or something; what's the matter?"

"You're a famous writer, what are you doing with a loser like me?" he asked. "I'm an ex-con.

"Yes you are."

"If I told you I was a big reader; would you think I was just trying to impress you?' James asked as he glanced at her.

"Yes," she laughed. "Well, maybe! Are you?"

"Yes and no; I don't read children's books like you write, but I do read; mostly mysteries, sometimes historical novels."

"I think that's great, I read a lot also," she paused. Should I tell him about my newest venture?

"You are so good at observing, at questioning people and things, I'll bet you could write a great mystery," he said.

"Wow, you read my mind, as a matter of fact, I've decided to write a novel," Athena said. "I've always thought about it but, since I'm now in the middle of one myself, it sort of grabbed me."

"I'll buy your first copy," James said.

"You'd better, you're my lead character!"

Hi mood changed abruptly. "You mean, all of this, introducing yourself to me, riding up here with me, it was just for research, to get some color for a book?"

"James, James," Athena said. "Yes, in the beginning it was. But the more I get to know you, I want to get to know you more."

He turned his head and gazed out of the window. Damn, she was just using me. And to think—

"—James," she said. "Look at me, please. What I see in you is that you're caring, you're sensitive, you are determined. Those are great qualities you don't find every day in a man. Those are the reasons I'm here."

They sat in silence for a few more minutes.

"James?" she said.

"What?"

"I'm here because I want to be here, with you."

"Are you sure?"

"Yes, I am," she said. "Here's how sure I am." She leaned in and kissed him, hard. Her hair brushed gently against him, and her lips felt like pillows. Oh God, he almost sobbed, it's been so long since I've felt like this.

He broke the kiss and stared at her.

"Wow," he said. "Wow."

He hunched over, hoping she wouldn't see what one kiss did to him. Wow yourself, Athena said, casting a sidelong glance at his lap.

"Um, ready to find a place to eat?" she said.

"I sure am," James burst out. "Oh, I mean, well—"
They both laughed at the double entendre.

She started the car. "Where to?" she asked.

"You had mentioned Ybor City?" James offered.

"Yes, sir," Athena said happily as she pulled out of the parking space. Something was happening here, something she couldn't control. The kiss was an impulse. But oh, it felt so good.

Soon they were in the heart of Ybor City.

"Look, there's a Mexican restaurant," James said. "Do you like Mexican food?

"I love it, maybe a margarita or two. This is a celebration, you know," Athena said with a smile. "Can you drink on parole?"

"My papers don't prohibit that, so I guess so," he answered. "I'm not a big drinker anyway, a beer now and then, but tonight we celebrate. It calls for a margarita."

The restaurant wasn't full and the waiter led them to a booth in the rear. By the time their drinks arrived the place was filling up. The music was loud and the people were noisy.

Athena looked around and started to feel something. James hadn't taken his eyes off her since they sat down, but that wasn't what she was feeling. She enjoyed the way he looked at her. Her uneasiness had nothing to do with James.

"James," she whispered, as she leaned towards him, "I think we are in a gay place."

"What do you mean," he answered, taking his eyes off her long enough to look around.

"Those guys walking in are holding hands and those two at the bar are practically making out on the stool."

"Wow! You're right. Well, we could make out too," he laughed.

She felt a delicious quiver go through her. But then, looking past his dancing eyes, she gasped. "Oh my God!"

"What," he whispered.

"Don't turn around, but do you know who just walked in? Deputy Tom Wiley. He's holding hands with a guy. They are definitely together."

CHAPTER 15: Friday, November 19

Sheriff Long eased his body into his chair. "I have to admit I am out of shape; I need to exercise more."

"OK old man, take a load off, I'll carry the ball." Keenan laughed, himself a little bushed.

They were tired from the door to door work of the previous day, but both men were in a different state of mind. The case had legs; but they were looking pretty hairy.

"OK, OK," Keenan said. "We'll work on a warrant. We can get equipment for shallow ground imaging. It can generate 2D or 3D images below the surface. Ground Penetrating Radar is not new, but has improved greatly in the past few years."

"I don't know anything about that, you're the expert," Sheriff Long said.

"I know you respect Parnell and heaven knows, I hope he isn't mixed up in this," Keenan said. "But right now, I wouldn't bet either way."

"Keenan, you been doing a good job with it," the sheriff said. "You prepare the affidavit for the search warrant and hope we can find a judge that doesn't know Mr. Parnell."

"Why, because you think they are all afraid of him?"

"Well sure, he is a powerful man, and he intimidates me and a lot of people around here, I'll admit."

"Sheriff, we have one chance to get this warrant right, that's my job," Keenan said. "But you are going to be the one to call Parnell."

"Damn, boy. I gave you this case, so you could make a name for yourself," the sheriff said. "I think you should do it."

"No way!"

"OK, we'll draw straws," the sheriff added.

"No, I'm going over to see Lola. I need to look at something besides your handsome face," Keenan said grinning. "I need something to eat; what can I bring you back?"

"I'll have one of those breakfast sandwiches; we can eat and work at the same time."

As soon as Keenan left the phone rang.

"Sheriff's office, Sheriff Long speaking."

"Hi Sheriff Long, this is Ken Bledsoe, how's it hanging?"

Bledsoe was the Hillsborough County sheriff. He and Sheriff Long went way back.

"Hey, Kenny," Sheriff Long said. "Good to hear your voice, you old he-coon. What's shaking in the big city?"

"Something just came to my attention and I need your help." Bledsoe said

"I'll try," Sheriff Long answered.

"We have a suspect in jail for armed robbery that took place last night." He paused. "The gun used to kill the gas station attendant was recovered. It is registered to Martin Filmore, deputy sheriff."

"What!" Sheriff Long's jaw dropped. Keenan breezed in, running his mouth, but shut up as the sheriff held up a finger.

"Kenny, I'm going to put Keenan McDuff on the other line—you remember him, right?'

"Do I ever; best road deputy I ever had. He still talking that Churchill crap?"

The men laughed as Keenan joined the conversation. Breakfast was forgotten as Bledsoe filled them in.

"Well, as I was saying, we have a suspect in custody in connection with an armed robbery. The gun he used was registered to Deputy Martin Filmore, from your office."

"You don't say, tell me more," Keenan sat upright in his chair.

"His name is José Vargas. He's a small time gang banger, strictly Tampa area, as far as I have been able to learn at this point."

"What's he saying, how did he get the gun?" Keenan asked.

"He isn't saying anything, he's already lawyered up. And listen to this. His lawyer is none other than Estefan Lopez from Miami."

"Wow. Maybe he isn't as local as you think," Keenan said. Lopez was a Miami drug lawyer, a high-priced string puller who kept his clients out of jail. "I need to find out more about the gun and how he came to have it. Is he alone in this? What else can you tell me?"

"There were two suspects, the other one is in the wind," Bledsoe said.

"Can I call you right back? I need to check something in my files. And Sheriff, thanks for calling." Keenan hung up as Sheriff Long and Bledsoe concluded their conversation.

As the sheriff hung up the phone, Keenan was already pulling out the accident report on Martin Filmore.

He laid the file on his desk, hastily flipped through it, and stopped at the part describing Martin's clothing.

"There it is. Why didn't I catch this before, it should have raised a red flag," he said.

"What's that?" the sheriff asked, after hanging up the phone.

"I think the fact that he still had his service revolver made investigators overlook the fact that his personal gun holster, the one he wore just above his ankle on his right leg, was empty."

"That's on me, son," Sheriff Long said. "I made a notation on the file. I guess I assumed it was at home." Sheriff Long shook his head.

"OK, how did a gang banger from Tampa end up with Martin's gun?" Keenan asked.

"Keenan," Sheriff Long said. He had a strange look on his face. "What if Martin's death wasn't an accident? This is going to kill Beth. My God, what's next?"

"A new investigation, I think," Keenan said.

"OK, call Bledsoe. You have to go that way to have the judge sign the warrant anyway," the sheriff said. "See what you can dig up, we'll set up the schedule for serving the warrant tomorrow sometime, those bones aren't going anywhere."

"Yeah, OK," he said, already returning the call.

When he turned around, Sheriff Long was staring at him.

"Take a look at this, will ya?" he said.

On the screen was the mug shot of José Vargas and his prior record.

"See something familiar?

There on the screen was a picture of a skinny Mexican, about five feet tall, according to the booking information. Keenan stared hard for a moment, and then it jumped out at him. The perp had a tattoo on his neck; a half moon with a devil's face.

Chills raced down his spine. "Sheriff—"

"—Wait a minute, Keenan," Long said. "This punk is only five feet tall! The man we are looking for is over six feet, built like a wrestler, and white as rice. This guy couldn't fight his way out of a paper bag without his gun and a tortilla."

"You're right," Keenan said. "But I don't believe in coincidences. What if there's some connection; what if this guy and the man Jake told us about are part of some sort of gang?"

"Yeah," Sheriff Long said. "Look, you have to go up to Vista to get that search warrant; why not make a trip up to Tampa to check out Bledsoe's suspect as well."

Keenan wolfed down his sandwich as he began gathering up his things.

"And, look, you're right, I'm the one who should call Parnell," Sheriff Long said. "I'll take care of it while you're gone."

* * *

The search warrant was a breeze, although Keenan knew he had set tongues wagging when he mentioned where it would be executed. Parnell was a name in the county, and the judge's clerk had gasped as the paper was drawn up.

This county will never be the same, he thought as he headed up to Tampa.

He knew the route by heart; he had driven it every day during his years on the Hillsborough force. But he hadn't reckoned on a jackknifed trailer clogging traffic. A one-hour trip wound up taking two hours. It was noon by the time he got to the Tampa exit.

He rocketed off of I-75 and into Tampa. He turned west on Tampa Express; traffic was a bear this time of year. Signs were up declaring Cigar Heritage Festival and the crowds were already forming. He exited on 22nd Street and was right there.

"Hey, Keenan," Captain Bledsoe said, as he saw his former employee come through the door. "You're looking good. Let's get right to my office," he said ushering Keenan in.

Keenan was pumped; he could hardly contain his enthusiasm. New details seem to emerge every day.

"Thanks for inviting me up here, Captain," Keenan said.

"Hold your thanks until you hear what I have to say."

"What's going on?" Keenan asked, looking around, remembering days spent in this office with his boss.

"José Vargas is dead."

"What?" Keenan felt as if he had been bitch-slapped. "No way. How?"

"Evidently he and another gang member got into it about an hour ago. The other guy had a shiv—where it came from, I don't know, but he stabbed Vargas three times right in the heart," Bledsoe said.

Something nagged at Keenan, but he let it go. His blood was up and he needed some answers. "I need to know how this punk got Martin's gun," Keenan said, sitting down.

"Sorry, I would have called you, but I just got the news myself. We're launching a full investigation into his murder, and several other issues," Bledsoe said. "I want to know how a low-life like him could afford Estefan Lopez, that hot-shot Miami lawyer. He packed up and left right after he identified Vargas's corpse."

"Tell me what you know about Vargas," Keenan said. "Also, what's with the tattoo? Is it a local gang thing? I've never seen it before, but I've heard about it once before."

"The only thing I know is from the Gang Prevention Department. It's a Miami gang sign, nothing local."

"Are you sure?"

"That's what they tell me. Look, I'm about to head down to the morgue to get the forensic report. You can come with me; after that we'll head over to the jail and see how the interrogation of the suspect in the Vargas case is going. "

Despite the warmth of the day, Martin wished for an overcoat as he and Bledsoe entered the chilly morgue. The attendants, who always looked as if they enjoyed their time with the dead, eagerly slid out a drawer that contained Vargas' remains. Death always shrunk people, Keenan thought, yet there was still something sinister, menacing, about the dead gangster. In an instant he knew what it was, the leering devil's face inside the half-moon.

"You said that tattoo is a Miami gang device," Keenan said.

"That's right. It's been around since Mariel," Bledsoe said, referring to the massive influx of Cuban criminals during the 1970s. "Every now and then we see one of these thugs up here, but it's predominantly a Miami thing. Funny, though, this is the second one I've seen in so many days.

"When did you see the other one?" Keenan asked.

"Well, I can show it to you right now," Bledsoe said. "It's on the neck of the guy who killed Vargas. Maybe his killing was part of some sort of power struggle."

Something in Keenan's mind clicked in. Years ago, he had watched a documentary about the assassination of President John F. Kennedy. He recalled how the alleged assassin was shot dead, in front of a phalanx of law enforcement officers, before he had been fully questioned. His murder left a lot of questions unanswered. As Keenan wrapped himself around that thought, he and Bledsoe approached the detention unit.

"There he is," Bledsoe said, as they stopped before a one-way mirror. On the other side was a scrawny white kid who appeared to be in his early twenties. Detectives were talking to him, but the kid was silent.

Bledsoe punched a button, causing a dim light behind the suspect to flash. One of the detectives looked up at the signal, then left the room to join the sheriff and Keenan.

"Anything yet?" Bledsoe asked.

"He's been like that all day, chief," said the detective, shaking his head. "He's dummied up; he won't even ask for a glass of water. He woulda pissed his pants if we hadn't dragged him to the john."

"Well, stay at it," Bledsoe said.

As the two men walked back to Bledsoe's office, the sheriff said, "Well, it looks like we're at a dead end for now. The kid in there won't even talk, much less ask for a lawyer."

"Could you give me everything you have so far?" Keenan asked. "I have to get back home, things are happening there on a five-year-old case." Keenan unburdened himself about the murder of the Jenkins family, which spiked Bledsoe's interest.

"Could you do me a favor?" Bledsoe asked. "Invite me down to watch the GPR; I need to learn more about it."

"Sure, as soon as I'm back. I'll have Sheriff Long call you. We'll probably get it started tomorrow," Keenan said.

After another hour Keenan walked out, not as excited as when he entered.

The ride home was filled with mental exercises. It was late, and Keenan was the only driver on the road. He drove along as miles of open land fell away from the road on either side of I-75. The sodium vapor lights cast a strange aura over the scenery, reminding Keenan of one of Ray Bradbury's landscapes from *The Martian Chronicles*.

Ah, me, he thought, as he began to even question his enthusiasm for the job. What was there to being a detective but a lot of dead ends? He thought about his relationship with Sheriff Long. Over the days they had pursued the case, he felt the old guy coming around. He had even given him a few compliments, wrapped in layers of sarcasm and understatement. That was a start, but Keenan hadn't gone into police work for pats on the back. He needed more. He needed a solid lead. But right now, he felt as empty as those miles of vacant land on either side of him.

He thought of what his hero would have said in such a situation. "Success consists of going from failure to failure without loss of enthusiasm," he said, repeating one of Winston Churchill's quotes. There had been a line of failures, a link of failures—something is tapping at my consciousness, he thought.

Mile marker 193, Jacaranda Blvd., flashed by, and with it came a shock of recognition. That's where Martin died, Keenan thought. What had he been doing up here? He thought of Beth, and imagined what his own wife would feel if something were to happen to him. His mind kept returning to Beth, to his last visit to her place—"Wait a minute," Keenan shouted.

He pulled off the road and got out his notebook. Martin was working the Jenkins case on the side when he died. The Vargas guy had a tattoo just like one of the men Jake said Frankie told him about. Could Martin have been going to Tampa because of a connection to the Jenkins murders? Any good detective knows the real value of hard work—if you push a case hard enough, the case starts pushing back, yielding up information that otherwise would have gone unnoticed. Martin's gun, for example. It re-established a link between the Jenkins murders and someone, maybe more than one someone, with the same tattoo as the possible perpetrators. Maybe Martin ran into one of the perpetrators, or an accomplice, when he died.

Hunches were a part of that detectives' luck—you followed a hunch, either up a blind alley or to a new clue. Either way, a good detective left no stone unturned, even if that rock was just a hunch.

Keenan thought a moment more, then cranked up the car.

First thing tomorrow, I'll head into the office to work on my hunches a little more, he thought. He wanted to make sure he had all his ducks in a row before bringing in the sheriff. Then I'll surprise the old guy by calling him over the weekend. Monday morning, if the sheriff agreed, they'd take a ride out to Beth's. Even in death, Martin may hold the key to solving the Jenkins case.

CHAPTER 16: Monday, November 22

"Wiley, we'll be out of the office for awhile," Sheriff Long said, as he and Keenan walked out the door. "Hold down the fort, will ya?"

"Where you goin', Sheriff?" Wiley asked.

"Um, we got a little business we need to take care of," the sheriff said. "Anything comes up, we'll be over at the Filmore place."

Keenan was already in the cruiser by the time Sheriff Long reached the vehicle. The men said little as they drove. Keenan was lost in thought. His experience on I-75 yesterday had filled him with confidence. For some reason, he felt that the visit would move the investigation forward. However, he doubted if Sheriff Long would get it if he tried to explain.

As they parked in Beth's drive, they noticed another car there.

"Guess who's here?" Keenan said, smiling.

"That's probably James, right?" the sheriff replied. "He don't waste much time."

"Well, after five years without a woman, I'd be moving fast too," Keenan laughed. "Funny, I remember when our office was his first stop every morning."

"Looks like that boy has found something a little better looking than us, hunh?" the sheriff chuckled.

"I think we can include him in on this discussion with no problem, OK?" Keenan asked the sheriff.

"Yeah, what the hell, he started this whole thing up, he might as well be in on the show," the sheriff said. He paused and gave Keenan a hard look before knocking. "That is, if there is a show."

"Good morning, gentlemen," Beth said.

"Good morning to you," Keenan said.

"Hi there, Beth," the sheriff said.

"Come on in, I've made a fresh pot of coffee," Beth said. "I know the sheriff needs his coffee early in the morning. Athena and James are in the kitchen."

The trio walked back to the brightly lit kitchen, where James and Athena sat, oblivious to the world around them. Things had changed since their dinner in Tampa. Athena and James sat down with Beth the next day and talked candidly about the budding relationship. Beth saw that the two had their eyes open, and that there was something there. And James, oddly enough, reminded her of Martin. He was just as stubborn, and even looked a little bit like him.

"Hey Sheriff, hi Keenan," James said, rising as the two men came in. "Athena said you-all would be coming over, so I figured I'd kill two birds with one stone and meet you-all here."

"Looks like the only birds I see around here are some love birds," Sheriff Long said. They all laughed as James and Athena blushed.

"Ah, Beth," the sheriff paused, "I need to tell you and Athena, face to face, that I was wrong to talk to you the way I did earlier, you know, about the investigation. Martin was a good deputy and, seeing James and Athena here, I'm reminded of how important it is for a man to have a good woman behind him. I know you supported Martin; you have a good head on your shoulders and Martin valued your help. So please accept this apology from an old dog that still needs to learn a few new tricks."

Everyone at the table looked anew at the sheriff. Suddenly, he wasn't the old retread who acted as if women should be barefoot and quiet. His grace in apologizing set a tone that would last through the meeting.

Wow, Keenan thought, now I see how he gets re-elected every four years.

"Sheriff, that's so sweet," Beth said. She actually hugged the lawman; now it was his turn to blush.

The sheriff's putdown last week still rankled Athena. Prior to the men arriving, James had been trying to convince her to give the sheriff the benefit of the doubt. She was glad she had listened to him and put her Chicago attitude on the shelf.

"Would you mind if we talked upstairs in Martin's office, Beth?" Sheriff Long asked.

"No, I don't mind, but it's not like it used to be. I've redecorated a little."

"That's OK," Keenan said.

Upstairs the light still streamed in from the east windows. But the room looked different, more comfortable, than it had the last time the sheriff had been there, right after the break-in. Now the room looked as if it had never been ransacked. Flowers, lace tablecloths, window sheers, and new throw rugs gave the place a homey, family atmosphere. But Martin's presence lingered.

"There has been some headway in the Jenkins case," Keenan said as they all found seats. "James, we don't have a lot of answers—yet. But, we have more questions, different questions and as the result of those, we have uncovered some other problems." Keenan looked down at his notes.

"Beth," the sheriff added. "We have tracked down a gun that belonged to Martin."

"I knew there was one missing," Beth said, moving toward the closet where Martin's gun locker was kept. "Here's the missing place. I gave you the serial number, do you need it again?"

"When was the last time you remember seeing it?" Keenan asked.

"Well, the night—the night—the last time I saw him," Beth said, starting to tear up. "When he left, he said he wouldn't be too long, but not to wait up, I didn't. While he was talking to me he put the gun, it was a Glock 17, in his ankle holster."

"You know your guns, huh?" the sheriff asked.

"Married to Martin, I had to," Beth said.

"The gun was used in Tampa; a suspect in an armed robbery had Martin's gun on him when he was arrested. Now we are trying to track the gun from Martin to this suspect," the sheriff said.

"Did the guy say where he got the gun?" Athena piped up. "Do you think he might have been responsible for what happened to Martin?

"It's not that easy," Keenan added. "This guy is dead."

"Oh," gasped Beth and Athena at the same time.

"You said he was arrested; when and how is he dead?" James asked.

Martin explained what had happened. James still looked a little mystified.

"Sheriff, can I say something?" James asked. "This may sound selfish, but I thought you were working my brother's case, I thought this was about him, I thought you were making headway."

"Well, this is confidential information…" Keenan looked at Sheriff Long, who nodded. "But that guy up in Tampa? He had the same tattoo on his neck as that of one of the men Frankie told Jake he had caught hunting on the Parnell property."

"What?" James said, sitting bolt upright.

"Yes, but now he's dead," Keenan said. "He died before we could interview him."

"And that's why we're here," Sheriff Long said. "We think Martin was working the Jenkins case on his own; we think that may have been why he was heading up to Tampa. Are you sure you've given us everything?" the sheriff asked Beth, "Martin was a detail man; he kept records like no one I ever knew."

"I gave you everything," she said. "All the files are gone now."

"Hey Beth," Athena said. "What about the Altoids box? There were a few jump drives in there; I forgot to check them out. Do you still have them?"

"I put the whole thing in the top drawer of the desk," Beth said.

Athena jumped up, opened the drawer, and held up the old tin box.

"Here it is! Let's check them now," she said flipping on the computer. "There are three jump drives here. You want me to do this?"

"Yes!" said Keenan and Sheriff Long at the same time.

Everyone moved closer to the laptop as Athena plugged in the first one.

"Look at him go; that's my boy" came a voice from the dead, Martin's, as he offered a father's biased play-by-play commentary on his son's football video.

"Oh, no," Beth began to cry, "Martin, Martin." She hugged herself. Athena immediately moved to her sister's side and wrapped her arms around her. "I'm so glad the kids left for school already," Beth sobbed. "I don't think they need to hear their father's voice right now, maybe sometime later."

"Ma'am, Beth, are you sure you want to keep looking at these?" Sheriff Long asked awkwardly.

Beth bit her lip. "Yes, yes, if you think it would help."

Keenan stepped over to the computer and closed out the video, "We don't need to play all of this. I'll try the next one," he said hoping it wouldn't be as emotional as the first.

On the screen was the recap of the Frank Jenkins case, this was the file that had started it all a few days ago.

"OK, we've seen this one, last try," Keenan said, switching the jump drives.

"Things are happening in my office that I can't explain," intoned Martin's voice again. *"They seem to*

be related (long pause) *I believe we have a bug in the office.* (long pause) *After I talk to my informant, I'll know who it is for sure. The informant just called, I'll meet him tonight. His name is José Vargas, a petty criminal from Tampa.* (long pause) *The most obvious is Long or Wiley, I don't think Wiley could do something like this, the guy just isn't smart enough. And why? It would take more,* (long pause), *knowledge than he has. Well I'm on my way. I just hope Vargas isn't pulling my chain."*

"Wait just a damn minute, I'm no bug, what is he talking about? What bug? This is crazy, I—"

"—Hold it, sheriff," Keenan said. "Did you hear that name?"

"You hold it; I'm going back to that office and rip it apart."

"Sheriff, sheriff, Martin just mentioned the same guy who was killed yesterday, the guy who had Martin's gun."

Beth gasped. The sheriff stopped in mid-sputter. "Damn boy, you're right. Can you take that thing back?—let's hear it again."

They listened to Martin's soliloquy one more time, then Keenan stood up.

"Look," Keenan said, "I might as well level with you all. This, what happened here this morning, was supposed to happen. Martin made it happen. Beth, I thank you for taking everything so well, but what I'm about to say may upset you—I apologize beforehand if it does. But last night, when I was coming back from Tampa, I remember thinking how, every time we had a lead on this case, it would fizzle up in front of us. Then I passed the mile marker on I-75 where Martin died and, well, it's hard to explain, but I felt as if he were talking to me. That's why we came here today, because I had a hunch that Martin—I'm sorry Beth—that Martin had something to tell us, to help us."

"It looks like you were right," Athena said softly.

"When you and Beth came into the office and said Martin had some information he had left, remember how your home got ransacked?" Keenan asked. He pointed at Athena. "When we went out to check up on that road you and James found, a contact we mentioned we'd be talking to had disappeared. And when I went up to Tampa to interview that robbery suspect, the one who had Martin's gun? He had been killed in what they said was a jailhouse fight."

"I don't believe in coincidences," Athena said.

"Neither do I, which leads back to the other message Martin left us."

"You mean, about the office being bugged?" James asked.

"Martin thinks I was the bug, no way," the sheriff said.

"Whoa, sheriff, I believe you," Keenan said. "What about Wiley? He's in the office now, alone. He could have done this, but I agree with Martin—he's not smart enough. And besides, what's in it for him?"

"Speaking of Tom Wiley, guess where we saw him last night?" Athena said.

"Athena, you want to tell them?" James asked.

"No, you go ahead," she answered.

"Well, last night after work, I had to go to Tampa to see my parole officer," James said. "Athena rode with me. We stopped afterward to eat." He looked at Athena and smiled. "I didn't see anything different about this restaurant when we went in, until we were there for a few minutes. Then Athena realized it was a gay hangout. I think I was the only straight one in there. Then Wiley walked in, holding hands with a good-looking young guy. He didn't see us; he hardly took his eyes off his date."

"Tom Wiley?" the sheriff asked.

"The one and only," Athena said.

"Sheriff, someone is using this against him could be forcing him to bug our office." Keenan said. "It's possible. Someone might have him in a honey trap."

"Honey trap?"

"You know, when a person sneaking around for sex is blackmailed or coerced into doing something," Keenan said. "What if someone else saw Tom one day with his lover and now has him under his thumb?"

"Yeah, but who—why?" the sheriff asked. His face was bright red and sweat beaded on his face. With his large white handkerchief he mopped his brow.

"Sheriff, Keenan, I'm not accusing anyone of anything, but…" James paused. Should I say what I'm thinking?

"Spit it out, boy," the sheriff said. "What's on your mind?"

"Well, Shorty knows everything about everybody in town, he acts like he is their best buddy, but his garage has more surveillance cameras than Wal-Mart."

"His garage?" Keenan asks.

"Yeah, and I think they are doing repairs that are not reported on the paperwork,"

"Why would you say that?" Sheriff Long asks.

"Because, I see the paperwork and I see the cars," James said.

"That's probably nothing."

"Yeah," James nodded.

"But on the other hand," Keenan said, "Why do that? Why do work that's not being recorded? Sheriff, think about it; Shorty's moving cars from Miami through here to Tampa. Maybe those cars are carrying more than rolled back odometers. Think about it, Martin was going to Tampa to check something out; Shorty's sending Wiley up there every week."

"Yeah, that's right, Wiley works for Shorty," the sheriff said, following the thread. "And I did see him fooling around with the AC unit a while back. I remember asking him how he knew to adjust the settings—he said it was something he picked up in the Army."

Beth, whose eyes were still red, sat there pulling herself together.

"You know, Athena, in the long run Martin is still directing this investigation," she said,

"Yes he is, and he would be very proud of you," Athena said. "Life isn't easy, but he knew you were strong, he will always be there to see you through. Don't forget that."

James loved that about Athena, her soft, caring side. He sat there numb with all he had heard and caught up in his growing love for her.

"James, James," the sheriff said, snapping him out of his thoughts.

"Yes—yes Sheriff Long," he said.

"I know you have some misgivings about telling us Shorty's business, but you know what'll happen if he's really involved in something bad."

James knew where the sheriff was going, but he didn't want to verbalize it.

"What do you mean?"

"If Shorty's arrested for any wrongdoing, there's a chance that you'll go right back to prison," Keenan said, picking up the ball. They were playing James, moving with lawmen's instincts to turn a chance into an opportunity.

Now it was Athena's turn to gasp. Instinctively she pulled James close. Her perfume wafted over James, which helped to make his next words easy for him.

"Sheriff, I'll do whatever you want me to do," James said.

"Good, stop by the office tomorrow and we'll discuss our plan," Sheriff Long said.

"The office?" Keenan asked "But—"

"Hey, champ, hold your horses," Sheriff Long said. "I may be old, but I got a little plan to smoke out some possums."

Athena's face clouded. She could smell a set-up a mile away. And James had just been sucked into working for Sheriff Long and Deputy Keenan.

CHAPTER 17: Tuesday, November 23

James was early; Athena knew he would be. His face was full of anticipation as he knocked on her door. She was ready. Athena had dressed in her newest designer jeans and silk blouse, and she looked sharp. James wasn't the only one anticipating tonight.

The ride was much more relaxed than their last trip together. They seemed to have found a common ground. She hadn't felt this much anticipation in a very long time. James looked at her with expectation, with enjoyment; he respected her as a woman and her feelings toward him were obvious. This was the first time she had been attracted to someone younger and it felt right. The age difference wasn't a factor. James made it feel right.

"Athena?" he said "I'm so happy to be with you. When I'm with you, I'm a different person. Do you ever get that feeling?"

"Yes, I do," she said.

"You know that old saying 'ten feet tall and bullet proof'? Well, that's me when I'm with you. When we are together, I want to be a better man, I want to see you smile, just because we're together."

Athena could only smile. What a great thing to say, she thought. "We do seem to hit it off."

"We're here," James said pointing to the steak house. Pulling into the lot, he parked in the rear, shut off the engine, and turned in his seat to face her. He put his right hand in her hair, pulled her face toward him, and held her as he looked deep in her eyes. His feelings for her couldn't be stifled any longer. He wanted to touch her, to hold her, to feel her heart beating against his chest.

"Athena," he said so softly that she could hardly hear him. She allowed herself to be pulled even closer. She started to say something, but at that moment his lips were on hers. His arms drew her into him, his tongue found hers; she melted into him and kissed him just as passionately.

Slowly he emerged, took a deep breath, let it out, and opened his eyes. "We had better get out of the car."

"You think?" Athena smiled, and didn't move.

"You first," he said.

Still she didn't move.

He reached for her again and the night was just beginning.

The atmosphere in the restaurant was casual; the smell of steaks and ribs whet their appetite. The waitress led them to a booth. James's eyes followed Athena as she moved. At the booth, he slid in beside her; his thigh felt hot touching hers. He felt warm all over.

"Look around," he said. "This is a family place."

"Yes," she laughed. "Not like the one you took me to last time." Remembering that night, she wondered what tonight would bring. Whatever happened—and she knew what she wanted to take place—she would be happy.

"I don't think I'll be able to think of Mexican food quite the same way again," James said, taking her hand and gazing into her eyes.

She gazed back at him, and wanted nothing more than to start the parking lot scene all over again. But she steeled herself and, instead, made some small talk. "How was work today?"

"Well, I'll tell you." He paused. "I have been a little worried about my job. Ah, not the job itself, but that Shorty is doing something illegal. You heard the sheriff and Keenan yesterday. I could get sent back and that's the last thing I want to happen."

"I've been meaning to talk to you about that." she said. "I think they were putting pressure on you, threatening you—I think they wanted you to do their work for them."

"I already am," he lowered his voice and spoke in her ear. "I'm squealing for them, I'm a stoolie, whatever."

"Oh James," she gasped. "Going back to prison is bad enough, but if you get hurt…"

"Don't worry," he said. "And don't repeat any of this, OK? Please."

"OK."

"I checked one of the cars, one that was ready to go on the transport." He pulled a pen out of his shirt pocket, grabbed a napkin, and wrote one word. 'drugs.'

Her mouth dropped open. "What?" she said, caught herself, and immediately whispered, "What?"

He only nodded. She was beyond surprised.

"What did you do?" she asked. From a distance anyone would think they were two lovebirds whispering sweet nothings in each other's ears. But the talk was no longer small; the conversation had made a mood swing from sexual to serious.

"What's going to happen next?" she asked

"Well, Sheriff Long and Keenan weren't real surprised, and they are planning a raid. First thing tomorrow morning; lucky I work afternoons," he replied.

"All by themselves? Won't they need help?" Athena was full of questions.

"Keenan is calling in extra troops," James said. "He used to work for the Tampa sheriff; they said he'd be bringing some people down. It looks like there may be a connection between Shorty's operation and drugs up there. I'm not sure about all the hows and whys, I only know it lets me off the hook

Athena's face mirrored her concern.

"Sorry if this upsets you," he said. "I'll make it up to you, I swear. You say when, you say how," he added, with that cocky smile she liked so much. She started counting the ways.

"I'm all right, just worried about you," she said.

"James?" a man with a pocked face and scraggly, unkempt hair said. "Just get up, nice and easy, don't make a scene and everything will be fine."

Athena and James both looked up; two large men were towering above their booth.

"Hey, what's going on, what do you want?" James asked.

"If you don't shut up and walk out of here, now, you'll be very sorry. Now move, you too, Athena."

Athena was startled, they know my name, they know James's name, who are these thugs?

Stranger number one inched his jacket back; James could see the butt of a pistol.

"Athena—" James said.

"We had better do what they ask," she answered.

They stood.

"Follow me," stranger number two said as he threw several bills on the table. Number one was right behind them.

No one in the restaurant was aware of the conflict playing out right in front of them.

It was dark outside, the smell of meat drifted out into the parking lot; James thought he was going to be sick. Athena must be going out of her mind, he thought, I've got to stay focused, for her.

"OK, what do you guys want?" James said, barely able to speak.

"You," the tall one answered, smiling.

"Athena, take the car, I'll talk to you later," James said.

"Not so fast, wise guy, she's going too."

"No, let her go. I don't know what this is about, but it doesn't involve her." James said.

"She's coming too, those are my orders," number one said, leering at Athena.

"Whose orders?" James asked.

"You'll find out."

The men forced Athena and James into a dark SUV and sped out of the parking lot.

James could tell they were headed south. What he didn't know was why. His mind wasn't on himself, but on Athena. If anything happened to her, the one person who believed in him and trusted him, he wouldn't be able to live with himself.

The car slowed down as soon as it passed the Mobil station. It turned left onto the overgrown road James had traveled his first day in Citrus City. They were on their way to the Parnell Ranch.

James didn't know if Athena had ever been there, but he could see she was scared. He wished he had told the sheriff where he was going earlier, he wished he knew what was going on, he wished he could protect Athena.

As they passed Frankie's abandoned house Athena started to cry, she knew where she was and it wasn't good. Just past the house, near the east pond, the driver parked the SUV.

"All right, just sit here, someone wants to talk to you," number one said and then gave a nasty laugh. Within a few minutes they saw headlights approaching.

"Out, both of you," number one said. "It's time to party."

They were pulled out of the car and pushed under an oak tree near a pond, as the other vehicle parked. Its headlights bathed them in a harsh glow.

Athena and James squinted with bewilderment. Like deer in headlights, James thought. Walking rapidly directly toward them with a gun in his hand was none other than Shorty.

"Hello, James, howdy, Athena," he snarled. "What's the matter, cat got your tongue?'

He rushed up to James. "I had a sweet operation before your sorry jailbird ass showed up," he screamed in James's face. Spittle flew as Shorty shouted.

"Out of all the hick towns in Florida, Frank Jenkins's brother picked this one. I figured keeping you close would keep you on a chain. Boy, I was wrong." He slapped James, hard. "You came to town and all hell broke loose. Boy, you are going to pay. Did you take a good look at that shack up the road?"

James couldn't speak.

"I'm sure you did. Remember your brother? Another meddling, good-for-nothing... Oh well, now you can be with him, both you and the little lady, here." Shorty waved his gun, and the gunmen with him began moving closer.

"Freeze," several voices yelled at once. "Freeze. Drop it or we will shoot."

Soon the three men were on the ground and handcuffed. James pulled Athena close as she sobbed. He was the strong one now.

CHAPTER 18: Wednesday, November 24

In spite of last night's arrests, there was still much work to be done in the sheriff's office, many loose ends still needed to be tied up.

Tom Wiley walked in; he looked like he had been run over by a Mack truck. And by day's end, he would wish he had been.

Keenan didn't look up; Sheriff Long watched Wiley's slow walk to his desk.

"Sheriff," Wiley said "Can I talk to you, alone, in the conference room?"

"Sure, I want to talk to you, too," the sheriff said. He followed him into the room and pulled out a chair as Wiley closed the door.

The room was littered with stacks of paper and the trash bin was overflowing with take-out coffee containers and greasy donut bags from the café. The paint was still peeling off the walls, but the room had new life, so did Sheriff Long.

"OK, shoot, what's going on?"

"I heard about last night. I'm real proud of what this office accomplished," Wiley paused.

"Cut to the chase, boy," the sheriff was in no mood to let this play out any longer.

"Sheriff," Wiley couldn't look him in the eye. "Let me say first of all. I'm sorry—sorry I let you down, sorry I let this town down."

"I know you are, why don't you just spit it out, you'll feel better and maybe I will too."

"I met a guy, a guy from Tampa," Wiley wasn't good at confessions. "I'm gay! I'm a faggot. I'm a queer. There, I said it!" His eyes were red, his tears were real. "I met this guy. I don't expect you to understand, but we really care about each other. Somehow Shorty found out about it. He took some pictures of us, well, some real bad pictures of us." His head was in his hands.

The sheriff handed him his big white handkerchief. Wiley blew his nose, and the sheriff made a mental note not to ask for the handkerchief back.

"I didn't know that the cars I was hauling to Tampa were filled with drugs," Wiley said softly. "That came later. Martin was nosing around and Shorty didn't like it. He wanted to know exactly what Martin knew. He forced me to bug the office. I hate myself for being weak; I didn't want to do it. But in the long run, I did everything he told me to do. Everything."

He looked at the sheriff, who stared back.

"After the bugging Shorty was king; he knew anything going on in town. One thing led to another, things started going from bad to worse. I wanted to tell you a hundred times. After Martin died, at first I thought it was just an accident, I thought it would end. You stopped working the case. Shorty could keep doing what he was doing, no one would know. Then James came to town."

Wiley was like a fountain overflowing. The words just gushed out, he couldn't stop them.

"When Beth and her sister came to your office, Shorty taped the conversation and sent someone to break in to their house just to scare them. It didn't work. There was the Philips boy—he's gone. Shorty is a terrible person and I know I deserve anything that I get. But I am truly sorry."

Wiley was spent. The sheriff reached over and patted the broken deputy's shoulder.

"I know you're sorry, I'll do what I can," he said slowly. "You will have to testify, and as far as you being gay, well gay or not, Wiley, I respect you for confessing, for taking ownership of what you've done, and for coming to me before I came for you."

Sheriff Long had tears in his own eyes. "We go back a long way. You'll be able to make bail, I'm sure. If not, I'll help. Sheriff Bledsoe has some questions for you too. He's going to take you up to Tampa later on today and book you there, OK?"

Wiley nodded. The meeting was over, Sheriff Long was exhausted. He needed another cup of Lola's coffee. He walked out the door and to the café without speaking to anyone. Frankly, he didn't think he could talk at all right now. Wiley's confession had set the tone for what would be a crazy day. The graveyard would surrender its secrets, bringing closure for a lot of people.

The pale November sun was already high in the morning sky and the café was full of old men taking up space. He ignored their questions, got his coffee, and made sure to get a second cup for his deputy. He knew he couldn't have broken the case without that redheaded know-it all, the one sitting behind his desk with his feet in the air. He smiled as he left the café, just in time to meet a caravan of lawmen. FDLE, DEA, and more alphabets than were in a dictionary were represented.

Keenan dropped his feet to the floor as several cars pulled up in front of the office. "Showtime!" he said softly.

The caravan to the Parnell Ranch attracted a lot of stares. Inside thirty minutes, they were entering the weed covered road to Frankie's house.

The professional group that emerged was ready for action. Sheriff Long left his cruiser blocking the road to the east pond. The weather was expected to be sunny and dry, which was normal for mid-November. The sandy soil would make for perfect working conditions. Ground penetrating radar used high frequency radio waves that were transmitted into the ground. When a wave hit a buried object, it is recorded on a screen attached to the unit and viewed by the operator.

"OK, I'm all set, ready to roll," the head technician shouted.

"I'll show you where to start," Keenan replied.

Everyone was quiet, it was a big turnout for a little town, and expectations were high.

"Hey, I think we have something!" exclaimed the operator. This was no surprise because the bone sticking out of the ground had marked the starting point. The screen showed the image of a body.

An FDLE man stuck the first small red flag on a wire rod in the sand.

"After Shorty began his confession, he filled in all the blanks," Keenan said as he and the sheriff stood side by side, amazed at what was happening.

"Yeah, Martin was on the right track all right," Sheriff Long added.

"Frankie was killed because of what Shorty thought he might have seen. I don't believe Frankie saw anything; if he had he would have told Jake. Jake didn't know anything about this." Keenan just couldn't understand such cruel behavior.

"Shorty said we can find seven bodies here, all were Miami thugs, gang-bangers," the sheriff said "Do you believe him? After all, he sold used cars."

Keenan looked around the area, if it wasn't for the secrets it kept it would be beautiful here.

"No, I've never met an honest killer, they always try to work the system, always hold something back to bargain with. The question is, what else will we unearth here?"

Once Shorty knew Wiley had turned, he began talking and hadn't stopped. They had the names of the three men who killed Frankie's family; all were members of the Diablos, a drug gang that used Shorty's vehicles to ship drugs from Miami up Florida's west coast. The FDLE, the DEA and the Tampa sheriff's office were all on the case now, and Frankie's murderers would be hunted down within the next few days.

Long was already thinking about tomorrow. I wonder how a press conference will be this time. I'll even let this kid have a speaking role. He smiled his campaign photo smile.

* * *

The sheriff had invited James and Athena to view the operation.

"I'm not sure I'm up for this," James said gazing around. Just the sight of a certain gnarled oak tree made him shudder. It was the very tree they stood under last night, waiting to be executed.

"I know, I was never so scared in my life," Athena said, holding tight to James hand. "I was worried about you. I knew you were thinking about your brother and the horror he and his family went through."

"I was thinking of you," James replied. "I wasn't going to let go of your hand, no matter what,"

"Did you know the sheriff and his men would be there?" Athena asked.

"No, I knew they had set a trap, I didn't know I was the bait," he said. Turning to Athena, looking at her beautiful face, he shook his head, "Let's get out of here, we don't need to relive this again, we have other things to accomplish before you disappear back to Chicago."

"OK," she smiled, "what shall we do?"

Walking to the car through the rough terrain, James said, "Mr. Parnell called, I have to meet him this afternoon. Will you go with me?"

"You think it will be all right?" she asked.

"I want you with me," was all he said.

Athena grabbed his hand as they walked to his car.

"I would like to make one stop," James said. They left the graveyard at the Parnell ranch and headed for the Baptist church.

Hand in hand they stood quietly near four graves that were covered with small blue flowers.

Athena saw tears in his eyes, he had such a tender side that it made her eyes water.

"The flowers are artificial," he said, "the real ones only bloom in the spring."

"They are nice, did you put them there?" she asked'

"I had it done," he replied. "They are forget-me-nots. They are a symbol of remembrance. I want Frankie and his family to know—I'll never forget them."

James seemed to clear his head; he looked off in the distance. They had just left one of the most gruesome scenes he had ever witnessed, but the church graveyard had a soothing effect. It remained a spot apart from that other world. But what about Athena? He cared about her; he felt responsible for what happened last night. If she would allow him to, he would try to make it up to her if it took the rest of his life.

"How would you like to come to Thanksgiving dinner at Beth's tomorrow?" Athena said, as the idea hit her.

"Are you sure you want me there? It's a family thing," James reminded her.

"I'm sure," Athena smiled. She began telling him about the blind dates her nephew, Taylor, had fixed her up with. She looked at James and blushed. "This time, I think I may have found a keeper."

Wow, James thought, it's as if she could read my mind. They held hands and seemed to look at each other for hours. James broke the mood. "Let's head over to meet Mr. Parnell."

The Parnell residence was south of the café. They turned right off US 41 at Mullet Bay Road. The large wrought iron gate with its dual security cameras seemed a little over the top. He stopped and punched in the 4-digit code which Parnell had given him when he invited James out to the meeting, and the gate swung open.

The palms along the drive were standing tall, swaying ever so slightly in the breeze. Looking past the huge house, he could see boats anchored in the bay.

"We're here," he exclaimed. "What a house."

Athena was impressed. He parked the car under the ivy-covered port-cocheré.

"This shouldn't take long," he said

The maid let them in and led them to the library. "Mr. P. will be with you in a just a minute," she said.

The well-appointed library offered several comfortable seating nooks. But before they sat, Mr. Parnell walked in.

"Hi, I'm Cleveland Parnell, you must be James Jenkins," he said offering his hand. "And you must be Athena Sands. Welcome. Let's go outside, the weather is much too beautiful to stay in."

Parnell led them to a patio under a giant live oak with a breathtaking view of Mullet Bay as a backdrop. As soon as they sat, he got right to the point.

"James, I am so sorry for your loss. Frankie was a good man. I'm sure you have been devastated by the terrible things that you discovered when you arrived."

"Yes, I was and I'm not sure if I'll ever be the same," James said. "We just came from the cemetery. I know you provided that for my family, thank you so much."

"It's the least I could do," Parnell said. "As you know, I live most of the year in Chicago."

"Yes, I know," James said "Athena lives there also."

"So I've heard," he replied.

"James, the reason I asked you to come over was because I need your advice," he said smiling.

"My advice?" Surprise registered on his face.

"Yes, I'm hoping to restock the ranch and make it operational again."

"That's interesting," James ventured, wondering where this was going.

"I've done a background check on you—"

"—You did what?"

"I would like to offer you a job," Parnell said.

"Me? Where?" Was he hearing correctly?

"The ranch, of course. Your brother's old job. It will be a couple weeks before the authorities are out of there, then we have to redo the fences, that house has to come down, but a mobile home would work there nicely." He gazed at James. "I left a lot of unfinished business here. It's time for closure."

James's mouth dropped open. This wasn't what he was expecting.

"Wow, all I can say is wow," he was almost speechless. "Can I think about it?"

"Yes, don't jump to conclusions. I'd say in about two weeks, I can start repairs."

Athena was as surprised as James, "Mr. Parnell, let me say, I think that is a great gesture," she smiled. "Not exactly the way I pictured you; but then again, you are from Chicago, and some great people live there." She laughed.

"Well, I'll be leaving in about two or three hours to head back there," he said. "If you want a lift, my Cessna seats 6."

"Well thank you, Mr. Parnell," Athena said. "But I promised my sister I'd stick around for Thanksgiving dinner."

The maid approached with a small note that she handed to her boss.

"Excuse me for a minute, I have to make a call," he said, walking toward the house.

"James," Athena said. "This is great, what do you think?"

"I think it's a great opportunity, except for one thing." He wasn't sure how to tell her, he wanted to be with her, only her. He looked at Mullet Bay at the boats moored there, all waiting, like him, waiting for a new chapter in his life.

"What's the problem?" she asked.

"You. I want to be with you." He paused. "I'm not sure if you feel the same, but, but, we haven't had a lot of time to get to know each other, yet."

Athena reached over and gently brushed a lock of hair from James's forehead.

"It's funny how things work out," she said. "Beth invited me down here to help her heal. She was devastated by Martin's death. But then you came along and, well, if you hadn't opened the investigation, Beth would never have found closure. Now she's ready to get on with her life. She knows Martin died a hero; now she and her family can have peace. Thank you for what you did for us."

James started to speak but Athena placed a finger on his lips. "You not only reopened the investigation, but you also reopened my heart. I have an idea; come to Chicago with me for a few days after Thanksgiving." She continued to sell her idea, talking faster as she warmed to it. "You've never seen the city, it's beautiful, the trees are colorful this time of year; people are friendly. What do you say?"

James wanted to yell at the top of his lungs.

"I'd like that," he said quietly.

Acknowledgements

Undertaking a project like writing a novel involves much help, most of which is given by many who may go unrecognized. To all who encouraged me, and to those who helped without realizing it, I offer my thanks. To my publisher James Abraham, I would still have unfinished business if it were not for your guidance and help. Thank you for being a friend and a mentor. And to my family, for their help and support and belief that I could do it, thanks.